LAND
OVER
TIME

LAND OVER TIME

SECOND BOOK IN
THE LYLE KENT SERIES

JUNE A. REYNOLDS

ILLUSTRATIONS BY: CLYDE LIST

TABLE OF CONTENTS

Dedicated to my mother, Millie Elizabeth
Wells-Weisenback, who, at the age of 97,
finally understands a writer's passion

Preface

By Lyle Kent

Dude. Don't get me wrong. I'm not a nerd, and I'm not pathetic. I'm a short guy who just wanted a normal middle-class life. But then I got caught in between a cul-de-sac, a war, and a recession and was ripped away from my own home. I had to make my way to an unknown place where some people don't like me.

All I wanted to do was escape back to my normal world, but when I got there, it too was changed. When I get away from people either in the desert or the forest, I realize that nothing changes—at least not very fast. I see kids doing drugs down under the bridge, and I understand their pain. I might be there too if I had the money or the time.

The town I live in is changing all the time. First, they cut down the little trees they planted near the sidewalk. Then they rip out the street. Then they plant more little trees. Then they rip them out again and rip out the sidewalk. Then they plant more little trees. All this happens in the course of two years. I can't stand it. No one else even notices, except for my great-grandpa. He keeps looking for the cherry blossoms to bloom on trees from one or two plantings ago.

Anyway, this life is all so crazy; and if it wasn't for my poor mom and my little brother and sister, I would check out, somehow. For their sake and for my great-grandpa, who has bailed me out of jail with probably the last war bond he had, I will try to do my best to stay sane and productive. This is the story of a land over time.

Of This Place

By Lyle Kent

Through this place came rushing water, rolling rocks,
and gushing mud.
Yes, this place was all laid over by the ancient ice age flood.

Man on two legs then came over; took some shelter
from a hollow tree.
Yes, this place was once walked over by the roaming
At-fal-i-ti.

Ferdinand Langer cleared the timber, grubbed the
brush down to the soil.
A hundred thirty-five years of farming, from the
family who did toil.

Through this place, the men came digging, when
Bodle's well was sucking sand.
Yes, this place became a river, saving fruit that needed
canned.

Rustic barn and field of walnut; island to the urban
sprawl–
Echoes from the well of time; listen to the trapped
cow bawl.

Through this place comes rushing traffic, rolling trucks, and spewing fumes.
Yes, this place could be all laid over, hardened off by asphalt plumes.

Now the bobbing clover trembles at the sight of wind and rain.
Soon to be all covered over, hardened off by pauper's pain.

The Get-Away

(Told by Two Points of View)

Quickly running out of the house, the teenage boy slammed the door behind him and dashed out to the road before someone came to the door wailing, "Lyle, Lyle, come on, let me go with you."

Lyle kept on going, backpack bouncing on his back, legs churning up the road. He passed mailboxes and signs, going east to the looming face of Parrett Mountain. It was a foggy day. The boy was reveled one minute, and then covered by swirling fog and mist the next second. Ground fog rose up all around the trees and drifted up the road, streaming towards the face of the mountain.

I was free, free at last to do what I wanted to do, and this was it! Running towards the fall forest, full of dancing colors of the leaves. Able to wander around and think...

There was a sudden roar of an engine, and a familiar old truck patched in black and paint was rounding the curve. It was Benny's uncle.

All I could think of was "Oh crap!" I had not seen Benny at all since I got back from our failed Arizona trip. The cops sent him back long before they sent me. I jumped into a ditch, hoping Benny's uncle would not see me. The truck swooped on by, fishtailing across the road from left to right. I cowered low in the ditch, hidden slightly by a few limbs of a young cedar sapling. I stared in the wake of the truck to see if it would come back or stop, but it was on its way to some other angry mission. I crept out behind the limb and sloshed my way out of the ditch. Now my shoes were all wet. Not the way to start a long hike. Urgently, I strode along the road, hoping that no one else came up the road, but that was impossible. Even though it was an early Saturday morning, several cars whizzed by—far too fast for a country road.

I had kept Benny out of my mind for a long time, but seeing his uncle today really got me thinking. I hoped Benny was alright. I kind of felt a bit responsible for getting him in trouble, even though it was his idea to run away with me.

I also still think about Benny's cousin Wade, who is handicapped. Benny's uncle was mad about me helping Benny learn how to change Wade's diapers. No one had taken the time to teach him. You just can't give anyone a job like that unless you teach him how to do it.

I walked up the long drive of Madge's farm, and then cut across at the walnut trees. I would not normally do such a thing, but Madge did not mind me doing that. I help her out with things all the time. She does not mind if I hike up here. Taking a deer tail that led up through the woods, I soon reached the base of the mountain where the rocks stuck out of the ground and the fault line rose up. I placed my hands on the rock wall, as if I had to make sure it was real. It was, but I never could believe it. A branch snapped, and I turned around. A couple of young does eyed me from the entrance to the woods, near an old apple tree, and followed at a distance out of curiosity. I sat down on one of the rock blocks and watched the deer.

My mom lowered the boom when I got back from Arizona last winter. She made me stay home and work. I was not allowed to leave the farm for anything. At first, I just cleaned up around the farm trying to cut the blackberry vines away from the old collapsed sheds, but our neighbor, Madge, got Grandpa and Mom excited about trying to get the grape fields up to production.

"They now have co-ops you can join where you can sell the grapes to vintners who make wine," she explained. "They will even come and pick them for you."

Grandpa exploded, "Co-ops! Why, I'm not joining some Communist conspiracy!"

Madge rolled her eyes. "Oh...my...gosh! This is not a political movement...this is farming!" exclaimed Madge, shaking her head. "It's just Walt, from up Chapman Road for God's sake! He does not have enough grapes for all the wine he needs to make. But he has all the equipment. You just sell him grapes by the ton. I'll teach you all how to prune the grapes this winter, and in a year or two, you will have some money for your work. Get Lyle out there. He owes you some money."

So I got out there in the field and learned how to prune the grapes. I had to pay back every last penny I owed to Grandpa for paying my bail and fines–at minimum wage. Rain or shine, no matter how cold, I was out there all winter. Mom took pruning lessons too and helped when the weather was good. She bought a Wi-Fi for our house, and I was able to finish the rest of the school year on my computer during the evenings. Finally, she gave one day off to do what I wanted for good behavior.

The slow-moving deer startled to a sound in back of them. The sound made their heads turn. There was more than one human out in the woods. The boy was quiet. The men in back of the deer on the trail were loud and crashing through the brush.

"Yup. This line goes right up through here, Todd. There's a two-hundred-acre rectangle here."

"I've seen enough, Paul. It's cold, and my shoes are wet."

"Don't you want to pace this side of the property off, Todd?"

"Naw, let's do it later. Someday when the sun is out."

"Well, that's not going to be for at least six more months, Todd."

Their voices drifted away, and the deer raced through the meadow to catch up with the boy sitting on the rock.

It was almost a year since I had been up here to the place where Madge and Grandpa told me about "Crack in the Wall." This year, since it was earlier, the ash trees were golden, and despite the fog, they shed a strange light. I walked through the light. Maples were turning gold, and the vine maples were red. For a guy from the desert, the colors of the trees are just strange and beautiful. I got to the waterfall, which was barely a trickle since the fall rains had not begun. I had the urge to go on further than before, following the rock wall of the hill.

Gusts of wind were swirling up to the wall and scattering a flame of leaves in every direction. All of the movements made me a bit dizzy as I walked along. The wind was wheezing a high-pitched song that sounded like it was coming from the wall. I spotted a young Doug Fir flapping its long branches back and forth, and I thought I'd stop near there and take a look. It was pretty shady this time of day, but I could see sunlight shining through the back side

of the tree. Without thinking, I pulled the flailing limb aside and stepped through the other side of the tree. It was warm on the other side, and the sky was completely clear of the fog. There was a well-worn path, so I followed it. After a quarter of a mile, the trail went down into a deep canyon. There were several strange-looking oak trees down there, right along the edge of the creek. They had heavy limbs bent out and up at ninety-degree angles, like they were pointing somewhere toward the east, the way I was going. Suddenly, looking at those trees, I got the shivers. For a moment, I looked back to where I had been. Where was the rock wall? I got a little nervous and thought about going back. But at the same time, I was on a wellworn trail. Not just an animal trail from the looks of it. Ahead I could see that it swooped around to the bottom of a creek bed and up the other side. I would at least go down to the creek. I continued down the trail.
Then I heard this:

> "Oway, Oway, tilly cont-tern!"
> Nay, Nay, Twalli-tum, Twalli-tum.
> Por Willi-mett?
> Nek-a Nek-a a wapatoe.

Voices from the top of the creek canyon from the other side!

I completely forgot all about the wall and turned back. This sound was so strange; human and yet guttural with grunts and clicks, I freaked, jumped over a log, and crawled down the creek bank into some sword fern. There were two people. I could hear quiet feet walking along, down the creek bank on the other side. I heard them splashing into the creek and walking up the other side. I peeked through the ferns. They walked by me by about twenty feet above, but they were preoccupied with some sort of conversation about where they were going. They kept pointing and flapping their hands this way and that, so I could tell.

After a second, I popped my head up when I thought they passed by. I caught a glimpse of two young men, nearly naked, with long dark hair carrying some rolled-up bark on their backs and strings of long slimy-looking fishlike creatures. The scent of these natives and their fish stayed in the air like a rotten rat in a barn. They continued on their way. I was shaking as I thought about the "Crack in the Wall" story, about the native boy who discovered it and used it with his family as a shortcut route to get to the Willamette River to catch eels for a few years. Then, the boy and his whole family disappeared according to the legend. Thoughts were racing through my head: *Who were those guys, and why were they here? Why am I here? Could I get back, or was I stuck? Was I lost?*

With great uneasiness, I got up and started back on the trail–under the pointing white oaks and back to what looked like the end of the trail. Everything looked the same, and I got a sinking feeling in my stomach. In a panic, I parted the underbrush, looking for the young Doug Fir branches. I was frantic with fear as I pushed the brush and ferns around. I was in a real panic, turning around in a full circle. Everything looked the same. The same. The same. Then I saw something dark and red behind a branch. It was the vine maples flaming beyond the fir tree! I plunged through the low limbs and found myself back in the cold foggy meadow. My heart was pounding. The grazing deer startled when they saw me appear from nowhere through the branches of a tree. They jumped a bit and turned their backs to me with their tails in the air. I just collapsed there in the cool grass. My heart was pounding. I started taking deep breaths.

When I finally got up, the first thing I saw was a rise of land with a little rocky knoll sticking up between the trees. It was calling to me. All I had to do is hike the rock wall to the end of the meadow. This is where I could go to think, like back in the old days in the desert. I headed toward the rocky crag.

21 Questions

It was pretty late when I got home. Teddy was on the porch looking like he had been there all day. You could tell that he had something to say.

"Where's Mom?" I opened.

"She went to the store. I stayed and took care of Grandpa all by myself! He's asleep right now," he bragged.

"Wow, Ted, that's pretty big of you," I said as I patted his back.

"Thank you." Teddy beamed.

"And where is Baby Mary?" I asked.

"Oh, she is with Mom. But I handled all the big important stuff while you were gone." He winked at me because he has seen great-grandpa do it so many times.

"Look, Teddy, I found a cool place where we can go. I'll show you the next time I can go there."

"Uh, okay. But you missed a pretty cool thing here," he said.

"Oh yeah, what's that?" I sighed. It was time for twenty-one questions with Teddy, the-four-year-old Kent.

He announced, "A stake man came."

"Oh yeah? Were they stakes for the grapes?"

"No..." He breathed.

"Did he think you were a vampire?" I asked.

He laughed nervously. "Of course not."

"Was he going to drive a stake in your heart?"

"No!" he shrieked.

"Were they silver stakes for a vampire?" Teddy chuckled.

"Noooooooo."

"Was he a Mormon from a stake house?"

"No. What's a stake house?" he asked.

"A Mormon church. Okay, I give up, Teddy. You win the game. Tell me what happened," I said as I sat down on a rusty old chair.

Teddy was ready to tell me the story. "So he was a steak man. He wanted to know if we eat steak."

"So what did you tell him?" I said.

"Well, I told him, we don't eat steak. An' he said, 'Are you a vegetable?'"

"An' I said, 'No, I'm not a vegetable.' An' he said, 'So what do you eat?' An' I said, 'Barbecued fireman chicken!'"

Just then, Mom drove up in the car, and I went out to help her with the groceries and Baby Mary.

"Did you have a nice day on your own, Lyle?" asked Mom.

I smiled. "Yes, I did. I hiked all day long. Thanks for letting me go."

Mom Goes to the High School

Right around the end of September, the phone rang one afternoon. I answered it. It was the counselor from the high school. She told me that the Star School's computer program was canceled because the state lost their funding.

"Do you still have your computer, Lyle?" she asked.

I lied (well, sorta lied). "No, it got stolen, sorry about that."

She sighed. "Well, don't worry about that, I guess. But that still means we must enroll you here at school. You don't want to be truant with your record, now."

My heart sank. There was no way I wanted to go back to that school after all the harassment I got there the last time. But I knew that I had to do something. Instead of holding my problems in and not being honest with my mom, I decided to lay it all on the table and work with my mother on this. I told her the whole ugly tale of last year. Her reaction really surprised me.

"This was all about small-town gossip. That's what this was all about," she hissed. "It isn't any better now than it was when I went to that school, Lyle. But we are going to hold our head up high and go into that school. We will set the record straight, and if we don't like what they offer us at any time, I will up and pull you out of that school, and you will be home-schooled."

I was not so sold on the plan. "I don't know, Mom."

Mom was determined. "This is a public school, and we have a right to send you there. Grandpa pays taxes for that school. They have a duty to educate you in a safe environment. We will give them one more chance to make this right. Do you hear me? I appreciate your honesty, Lyle. We will try to do the right thing. I think you are college material, and I want you to be successful."

So the next week, Mom was in her "Kent Family Flash Mob" mood when we went to the high school to register. Even though Grandpa offered to babysit, Mom refused and took Baby Mary and Teddy with us. No doctor's office, food stamp line, DMV, VA lobby, dentist office, or counselor's office today was safe from the search-and-destroy tactics of these two terrible toddlers. All wastebaskets would be emptied or filled, forms crumpled, magazines licked, chairs climbed and toppled, and crackers sprinkled across the rug. The longer they made us wait, the more devastation.

The counselor's office was devoid of baby toys, so the terrible two headed for the brightly colored college information table. Baby Mary, who could walk now was the master of clearing a table with one swoop of her chubby baby arm. Teddy, who liked order was picking up the catalogs and ferrying them across the room to me. Suddenly, Baby Mary grabbed a freestanding lamp wire that came crashing down. She started to wail. Quickly, the receptionist made a phone call, and we were whisked into the main office of the counselor. While Baby Mary gummed a U of O catalog and Teddy ate fish crackers, Mom and I chose classes based on the Star School transcript from last year.

"Wow!" said the counselor. "I think you should take advanced English, Lyle. Look at these stellar scores in reading and writing."

Mom shook her head. "I don't know. Maybe he should just take easy English."

"He will be bored, Mrs. Kent," said the counselor. "He looks like college material to me. I think letter writing and filling out applications is not enough for Lyle."

"Well, what do you think, Lyle? Could you handle that?" asked Mom.

"Maybe," I said uneasily. It was the first word I said since we got there. "I'm pretty good at writing a story, and I read everything I can get my hands on, but what I'm really worried about is that kid, Calvin. Can I just not get any classes with him and his buddies?"

"Calvin is no longer with us. In fact, he and his buddies started a fire down on the old Tannery property, and they all are studying at Donald E. Long this year."

Donald E. Long was not a school but more like a juvenile detention center. I had been threatened with that myself when I came back to Oregon. Now I really knew I'd have to "stay on the straight and narrow" as great-grandpa put it.

Back on the Farm

On the eighth of October, which was a Saturday, we woke up to a crisp frosty world. Teddy looked out and yelled, "Snow! Snow!"

But of course, it was not snow, it was a thick layer of ice. There was not a cloud in the sky and soon the sun splashed its warmth over the vineyard, and the frost disappeared. The vineyard had turned from green to gold in one night, and the golden grape vines were glowing in the sun. I could not take my eyes off the sight. I sat down at the kitchen table and wrote this poem in my writing journal:

The Change of Days...

Comes upon you, almost like a
ghost that wants to surprise.
Or
In a flash before our eyes, the
humbird's plaintiff cries.
Shocking colors and shapes of distressed flowers.
And
High-gathering clouds in booming towers.
Add
The launching of a thousand geese,

The swirling fog of inner peace,
The single frog who still complains.
Days grow shorter with this change.

Yes, days grow short in this change.
There is no lingering here,
For the Change of Days is sneaking up and is near.
And you must change your ways.

I sort of wanted to edit the poem but was interrupted by a horn honking. Then Madge was pounding on the front door. I opened the door to her booming voice. "Wow, Lyle! Your grapes have changed color! Mine haven't yet. I called Walt this morning, and he came down off Chehalem Mountain to see what you had out there." While she was saying this, her recently highly mobile twins were racing around our front yard. Teddy squeezed out the door with no coat on, and instantly the three were chasing Walt's Col lie around the front yard. Walt came loping up the drive.

"Sorry to bother your folks so early, but the grapes are not going to wait for us." Chuckled Walt. "I've been wanting the Pigage strain for a longtime. I'm so excited that your grandpa has help getting this vineyard back together." Grandpa and Mom came out with their work clothes on and Teddy's coat, and we all went out and looked at the vineyard.

The vineyard was glowing golden, and the grapes were dark reddish purple and hanging on in contrasting blobs. I had no idea that there were so many on the vines.

Walt looked around and went up and down a few rows. Mom nervously pulled weeds that were going to seed. "You've done a great job of pruning," said Walt approvingly. "You need to get rid of some of these madrones. They are just like weeds, sucking up the water the grapes need. The weeds are water suckers too especially those right around the trunks of the vines. If you mowed the grass and weeds and kept them down in the aisles, you don't have to do too much with them. I reckon we can get maybe a half a tote this year, which would be about five hundred pounds. Next year, you might get three thousand pounds. We could do a 'Pigage' label. This year we will make a blended wine."

Then Walt folded his arms. "So my next question is, 'Do you want me to bring in pickers and charge you, or do you want to do it yourself?'"

"I think we could do it ourselves," said Grandpa. "If you show us how."

"I'll help too," said Madge. "And then you can come and help me."

"That sounds great," said Mom.

"Okay," said Walt, shaking Grandpa's hand, and Mom's, and even mine. "We are partners. I have some paperwork in the truck for you to fill out and sign. After that, I'll go back out and test the grapes." Walt turned to me. "Do you have time to help me do some testing, kid?"

I was beaming. "Sure."

Racing the Weather

We waited another day to let the sugars go into the grapes with the sunlight. We were nervous, checking the weather on the Internet every hour, and Walt called us that night. He said that everything was ready for us to do a pick, and since we elected to pick ourselves, he could get his hired workers to do his crop while he helped us learn the process. We went to the hardware store on Sunday and bought five pairs of clippers and some gloves, so we were ready.

Walt pulled up the next day with two tote bins on his truck, and we off-loaded them near the field. We each took a row and our clippers and a white Saturn bucket and started clipping bunches of grapes off the vines. Teddy worked with Grandpa in the morning and with Mom in the afternoon. They traded off watching Baby Mary. Madge came down too. By afternoon, it started to sprinkle, and grandpa came out with some blue tarps to put over the totes. Everyone forgot that it was Monday until the school bus roared by on Highway 99.

"Mom, you'll need to call the high school tomorrow and excuse my absence." I reminded her. Naturally, we did not finish, and I missed two more days of school. We each worked feverishly in the rain, running back and forth with more buckets from Walt.

By 1:00 p.m. on Tuesday, we finished the first tote, and Walt brought down the forklift, loaded it on the truck, and took it away. We ate some tuna sandwiches right out in the field and kept on working. It was raining pretty steady by then, and we didn't want the grapes to get wet, split, and start molding. We were still not done by Thursday, but Mom made me go to school, only to find out that school was only a half day because of statewide teacher in-service.

I decided to walk home so I could hangout after school, get my homework, and also talk to Mrs. Bricks in the library. When I got home, the forklift and totes were all gone, and the harvest was over.

The next week, we did the same work over at Madge's farm.

Used-Wood Business

We didn't mean to, but grandpa and I started a new business: A used wood business. We were trying to get the tractor out of the old lean-to barn. I had already tried to cut away at the blackberries. Now with the grape harvest in, we decided to go back to tearing down this building. I would untangle the old wood and drag out chunks of it to a pile. Grandpa and Teddy would take out or pound in all the nails. Teddy got his own hammer, which he took to bed with him. This shed was the nearest one to the road and one day one of our neighbors stopped his truck on the road and asked what we were doing.

"Hey" he yelled over the engine of the truck, "I can pull on a few of those beams with a chain from an angle and get that old corrugated zinc roofing to go to the side and not crush your tractor or your kids." He pulled the whole shed apart in two hours, exposing the tractor to the elements, but it was out. Later the same guy came back with three old tarps and we stopped our work to cover and stake down the tarp over the tractor.

While we were doing this, another man and lady came by and asked about the old wood. They wanted to buy it for art projects they were working on.

Grandpa's eyes twinkled. "Five dollars for a pickup load." He said. "Come and get it whenever you want."

They took a load right then and there because they wanted to get it under cover so that it would be dry. The next day, the man came back for another load and gave Grandpa a sign made from his own barn wood that said: "Old Man Lowe's Used Wood" We staked the sign right by our demolition project.

Back at the School

It was hard to believe that I was back at the same school as last year. The very first thing I did when I got back was to take my overdue library books back to the librarian, Mrs. Bricks. She acted like she saw me and the books just yesterday. I apologized about their lateness and promised her if she made me a list of books that she needed and told me how much I owed her in fines, I would buy the books myself from the bookstore, at Powell's, in Portland. She thought that was a great idea.

Sophomore classes were much more interesting to me than the freshman classes but not any easier. In AP English, I had two novels to read; one was a summer novel we were supposed to read during the summer, Conrad's *Heart of Darkness* and the current one, *To Kill a Mockingbird* by Harper Lee. I had to read both of the novels for the semester final. I came back to school just as they were studying free verse poetry, so I had some time to get my act together. I also had Biology, US History, PE, and Home Economics.

On the second day, I was in line for breakfast when someone tapped on my shoulder. "Hey, excuse me, uh, hey... Uh..." It was my old friend, Benny.

"Hi there, Benny!" I exclaimed. It had been almost a whole year since I met him the first time. It looked like he grew about three inches. Next to him was his cousin, Wade, with his Jack-O'-Lantern smile, clapping his hands and greeting me. Wade was handicapped, but I could tell that he also was growing in other ways. I was so happy to see those guys, and they were too. It was all we could do to keep from hopping up and down and hugging each other. We knew that we had to be cool though because we had gotten into a lot of trouble last year and didn't want to make any bad impressions.

In AP English, no one wanted to sit by the windows for some reason. There were two rows of desks by the windows and only one girl sitting there. To be safe, I sat in the second row from the windows. We had a lecture from Mr. Painter about William Stafford, who was so great a poet that he became the poet laureate of Oregon. Man, I thought that sounded like a cool job, running around the state reading your poetry and publishing books. Mr. Painter read us about a dead deer by the side of the road. Some of the girls cried, and the boys snickered. It was a common scene in Oregon, and yet the description made it seem less ordinary.

"Now" said Mr. Painter "I asked you to take a common thing and make it less common through poetry. I know you boys over here had a late practice last night, but hopefully you came up with SOMETHING..." At this point, he ogled his eyes at a bunch of football players who sat by the door for easy bailout. "I want you to find a partner and exchange your papers. You and your partner will be writing notes on these two (count 'em) TWO sticky notes. You will have fifteen minutes to read and report on the sticky note...GO."

I looked around me, and everyone seemed to have a partner. I looked over at the window, and the girl who sat next to me just sat there, staring at her paper. She had hers all typed out, and it looked like quite a few lines.

"Umm, hi, I'm Lyle," I said as confident as I could.

She whispered with her eyes still on her paper. "I'm Janice."

"Do you mind being my partner? I, uh, don't have mine done, er, it's not the way I want it, anyway. I could use some ideas." At this point, Mr. Painter came over and slapped two orange sticky notes on my desk and two pink ones on Janice's desk. Janice looked up at the teacher. As soon as he turned around, she grabbed up her two pink sticky notes and traded with me.

She sighed. "Okay, I guess you can be my partner, but just remember: I hate pink!" She plunked her poem down on my desk and grabbed mine. This is what I wrote:

The Trees
Swathed in their summer robes,
They fall, as a golden vain-glory call.

Our eyes see the gilded hue–
And then they are standing quite true,
Naked to the cold world of winter.

The bell rang, and Janice slammed the pink sticky notes on my desk with my pitiful poem. On one she wrote: "TOO MUCH RHYMING" On the other she wrote: "NOT LONG ENOUGH"

On her orange sticky note I wrote: "GREAT THEME AND RHYTHM" Her poem was so perfect, I could not think of anything to say so on the other note I wrote: "REMEMBER: NONE OF THESE STICKY NOTES ARE PINK! IT IS AN OPTICAL ILLUSION!"

The Stuffed Shirts

That same day, I came home from school and found grandpa in the front yard with two big fat-looking slobs in suits. When I got close, I realized that these guys looked like brothers, and that one of them looked exactly like the guy that Benny and I ran into at the library/city hall building over a year ago, who told us to get a good education, and we could become mayor of this town one day. That guy did sort of look me in the eye like he recognized me.

Grandpa kept saying, "No, no, I'm not interested. I think you should go. No, no, I'm not interested." They acted like Grandpa was crazy, but Grandpa has been taking pills to make him more lucid, and he is pretty healthy these days.

Finally, the men shrugged their shoulders and tromped away to their black cars, which were eerily identical.

I scratched my head. "Who the heck were those guys, Grandpa?"

Grandpa's voice sort of cracked. "Oh, oh, those were just some lost guys..."

"Oh yeah? They looked like they were trying to sell you something," I commented.

Grandpa snorted. "Yeah! A bill of goods."

Later that night, over dinner, Grandpa told us that the "stuffed shirts" who came to visit him were from the school district, and that they wanted to buy Pigage to build a new high school.

"A new high school?" Mom exclaimed. "The one they have is pretty big and new, that seems foolish!"

Grandpa shook his head. "I don't know, that's what they said."

Mom turned to me. "Lyle, has anyone at the high school said anything about building a new high school?"

"Nope," I said. "I've never heard a thing about it, but I'll ask around."

Shad

The next morning when I was in line for breakfast, I asked a couple of people about the new high school. Three said they never heard of it and one said, "I do not give a rip."

There was a new student at school. His name was Shad, and he was staying at his Aunt Madge's house. Madge brought him by one day while we were tearing down an other shed, and Madge volunteered him to help us. He was a junior in high school and highly opinionated. The first morning he enrolled, he came and sat down with me in the lunchroom. He didn't see Benny and Wade until it was too late for him to avoid us.

I greeted him. "Hi, Shad, this is Benny, he's a freshman, and this is his cousin, Wade." Wade started clapping.

Shad stared at the two boys through his long straight blond hair. "Okay." He breathed.

"Hey, Shad," said Benny. "Are you a rock and roll singer? 'Cause you look like one."

"Nope," informed Shad.

I thought I'd start some sort of conversation. "Shad is from Gresham High. He's staying with his Aunt Madge."

"Wow! Gresham's on the other side of Portland!" said Benny. "The bus line in Sherwood goes all the way to there and back."

"Yeah, man," said Shad, as he rolled his eyes. "I see that you are not geographically-challenged."

Benny was embarrassed. "We've gotta get to class early! See ya!" Benny picked up the trays and guided Wade away from the table.

"Man," said Shad. "Those guys are kooks!"

"Yeah," I said, trying to be nonchalant. "But they are funny, lovable kooks. Did you have a good time tearing up the old shed on Sunday?"

"Yeah," said Shad. "I love destroying things."

"Pretty soon we will be back to pruning grapes. You can pretend you are chopping off arms and legs." I grinned at him.

"That sounds okay," said Shad. "But I think your old man would be better off if you guys just got rid of all those grapes and planted marijuana. You'd make a heck of a lot of money."

I started laughing nervously. "Hey, that's illegal. I've already gone to jail, and I don't want to go back!"

"Big deal," said Shad. "That's why I'm here. I got kicked out of school in Gresham for dealing. Imagine my delight when I got sent to Sherweed!"

"What?" I croaked as I choked on my toast. "I've never heard that."

"Oh yeah," he said. "It's all over the state. Everyone calls this place Sherweed. It's supposed to be known for the medical stuff."

"Well, that information is new to me, and I've been around for about a year, all together," I said, shaking my head.

Shad stood up from the table. "I gotta newspaper article to prove it. Pamplin Media don't lie, man. I'll bring it tomorrow 'an school ya." Then he flipped his hair out of his face, grabbed his tray, and walked away.

Shenanigans in the Library

The 7th period bell rang, and I took off for the library. I had some work to finish before walking home. There seemed to be no one in the library. Mrs. Bricks was not at her desk, and the aide was nowhere to be seen. I could hear someone moving around in the stacks though, and they were getting louder by the minute. After about five minutes of distraction of tittering, whispering, and giggling in the corner of the library, I got up to see what was going on. There was Wade and Benny, laying on the floor snickering over some book they were looking at as they hid in the stacks. I thought at first that it was a big cartoon book, but then I saw by the pictures that it was some sort of health book.

"Hey, Benny! Hey, Wade. What are you doing? Shouldn't you be getting on the bus?" I questioned.

Benny jumped up. "Oh, man! Did the bell ring? We gotta go, Wade!" Wade was still laughing and looking at the book. They darted out the door. I saw that the book was titled, *Our Bodies, Our Selves*. The picture they were looking at was a pretty graphic illustration of sex organs. I took the book up to Mrs. Bricks at the desk, and I left it there. Then I finished my writing.

Coyote

by Lyle Kent

Coyote was making his way across the desert. Zigging one way around a stand of cactus, zagging another way around the rocks. He found Prospector Trail and followed his nose to the Whiskey Wash Bar. He decided to go in. It was as dark as a cave. His eyes got used to the dim light, and he hopped up to the bar and put his paws on the flat wood.

"What can I do fur ya, stranger?" said the barkeep.

"I'll have a drink," said Coyote.

Well, this was Whiskey Wash Bar, so when a customer says they will have a drink, that means they would want whiskey. So the barkeep gave Coyote a shot of whiskey.

Coyote lapped it down then said, "That little bitty glass was not enough! I want a saucer!"

So the barkeep gives the Coyote a saucer of whiskey.

Coyote laps it up. The water was burning like fire on the coyote's tongue. He was so thirsty that he fell off the barstool and crawled out the door.

"Hey, wait a minute, pard'ner," yelled the barkeep. "In this saloon, you gotta pay!"

"Ah, and did you pay the clouds for the water?" asked Coyote.

"No," said the barkeep, without thinking. Everyone else laughed.

Coyote walked outside on that note. That was the worst tasting water he had ever drank. *What is wrong with this place?* He thought. It really was not like the desert. He wished that he could go back to the desert. He almost ran into a saguaro because he was blinded by the sun. He forgot he had been in a cave; it was so bright! He wandered around up and down many paths with tin tipis on either side. "Look at that scroungy dog!" said a little girl. I am NOT a dog, he thought as he trotted along.

The sun sunk low into the mountains and soon the sky was purple and dark blue. Coyote came to a fence, and on the other side, there was grass, sand, and a pool of blue water. He climbed through the fence. Coyote rolled in the grass, did his business in the sand, and then jumped in the pool of blue water. A man yelled, "Watch out, Walter! There's a Coyote in the water hazard! Get the groundskeeper, Bill!" The men jumped up and down and waved sticks with funny round mallets on the end. Coyote ignored them and drank the water. He stood in the water and let his fur get all wet. It was cool, and when he got out, he took half of the water with him. Soon there were all the yelling men and a groundskeeper in little carts that puttered around as they chased Coyote all over the grass and sand, until he found a hole in the fence that went out into the desert.in little carts that

puttered around as they chased Coyote all over the grass and sand, until he found a hole in the fence that went out into the desert.

I am not thirsty anymore, but I sure am hungry, he thought. Then he saw a fat rabbit. "Rabbit," he said. "How did you get so fat?"

The rabbit did not trust the Coyote, but he told him her secret anyway, "I sneak up to the man's porch each night and eat the dog food put out for the dog."

Coyote nodded. "Oh," he said. "That sounds like a very good idea." He only said that to put the rabbit at ease. He had no intentions of going back to eat at the man's porch. He knew that rabbit, by habit, would go her way, but circle 'round to see if Coyote took her up on such an idea. So Coyote turned back just a bit to see if the rabbit would also circle around, and when she did, Coyote leaped in the air, came down on the rabbit, and ate her.

After all was digested, Coyote took a bit of a nap. That water at the bar not only made him thirsty, it also made him sleepy. The whole night he slept under a mighty saguaro with many arms.

The next morning, he woke up to the doves cooing. The sun was rising through a prism of puffy clouds. He looked up to see a blazing white church. The lighter it got, the brighter the church became until it looked like it was on fire! He was so weak and dizzy he could hardly walk. He knew if he could get past the church, there was a cafe where he could order menudo to calm his stomach and head, so he dashed over the rocks and past the flaming church to a wide hard road where cars were whizzing by, and then...

I woke up and sat bolt upright in bed. My pajamas were soaked with sweat, and the sheet felt like ice. The wind was pushing a vine maple tree up against the cracked bedroom window. Gusts of rain were slapping the window and roof in time to the wind. It was in the middle of the night in Oregon, and I was having one of my Arizona dreams. There was no way I was going to get back to sleep now.

Outside Influences

It was a typical Wednesday at lunch. First lunch was over, and second lunch was just starting.

I walked in a little late. There were many people in the lunch line, so I was glad that I had a lunch bag today. I just walked over to a corner of the cafeteria and sat down by the windows. The kids from special ed were shuffling out to the lunch line too. My old buddy, Wade, Benny's cousin, was not with the group, which I thought was unusual. I rummaged around in my lunch bag for the sandwich, but it was just dry old peanut butter and no jam. The apple made up for the sandwich.

Suddenly, out of the corner of my eye, I saw Wade outside the window, scrounging around through the bushes like he was looking for something. I thought that was unusual, even for Wade, but no one, including the aides, noticed him.

The lunch line rapidly spread out to the tables. I heard the glass doors slam, and suddenly the huge room got really quiet. When I looked up, I choked on my sandwich–there was Wade, zombie-walking right up to my table, holding a rifle! He was panting. "Kkkk-yyy-le, you are evil." He breathed.

I stood up in shock. "Wade, what are you saying?"

He held the gun straight up in the air. "You, rainbow boy. Dad says you die." His eyes were red, like he had been crying. He tipped the heavy gun straight in the air, and everyone screamed. There was a rush of scuffling, and Wade looked around the room. By now everyone was under the lunch tables. Waving the gun in the air, he looked around and saw everyone laying low, and I could tell this made Wade feel very powerful. He cried, "Dad found my book... and it is all your fault." I had no idea what he was talking about at first. But then I recalled our last meeting in the library.

Then out of nowhere, Benny appeared. He spoke in a smooth, soothing manner, "That is not true, Wade. We got that book at the library. You promised to keep it in your locker, remember?" At the same time that Benny spoke, he moved toward Wade, who was still holding the rifle pointed up in the air.

Wade burst out in tears. "I know, I know, Benny, but I couldn't help it. The book... special. I wanted to take it home...have it in my room. But then Dad found it..." The gun was getting heavy in Wade's arms. He was sobbing. He tipped it toward me, but then he shifted his legs, and the rifle tipped the other way toward the windows. His arms were tired holding the gun. Benny reached out and grabbed the gun, but it went off, shattering the windows. The gun clattered to the floor, and Benny lay on top of it. Glass was cracking everywhere, all the people in the cafeteria were on the floor, except for me and Wade. Wade let out a wail and collapsed on the floor, crying as three cop cars with red and blue lights flashing pulled up outside the cafeteria.

The cops moved in like a SWAT team with their guns. "Down, down, everybody, down!" they shouted. I was the only person who was not down, so they arrested me. Then I passed out.

When I came to, I was in a squad car. I could see Wade in another car. Benny was waving at me in another cop car. I looked around and saw that all the lunch people were streaming out a side door. It took the rest of the day and far into the night before the cops had my mom come and get me.

Another Day of Grilling

But that was not all. The next day I had to go back to the cop station with my mom to a hearing or meeting or something. Possibly investigation. I'm not sure. There we were, in a room with me, my mom, Mrs. Bricks, who was my "child advocate," and a counselor.

The main cop didn't waste any time. "So, Lyle, why do you think Wade wanted to shoot you?" I told them the whole story about Wade and Benny in the library with the *Our Bodies, Ourselves* book. Mrs. Bricks sat up and said, "They were there by themselves?"

"Yep. There was no one else in the library, and the door was open," I explained. "They didn't even know the last bell rang, and they might miss the bus."

The cop took over. "So did you give them the book?"

"No. They left the book on the floor, and I put the book at the check-out desk, like you are supposed to," I said.

The cop's eyes narrowed. "So did you have any more encounters with Wade or Benny over this book?"

"No I did not," I answered. "In fact, I didn't even talk to them for at least a week."

Another cop started grilling me. He must have been the "Good Cop"–he sure had a smooth voice. "Sooo, uh, Lyle, can you explain to us why and possibly how Wade decided he wanted to kill you?"

So much for the soothing "good cop" approach. "I have my theories," I said. There was silence.

"Surely you have some idea," said good cop. There was silence.

"Oh, for God's sake, Lyle," said my mom, who was checking her watch and hoping to get back to a half-day of work. "Tell them the truth, Lyle. Tell them about the outside influences of Wade's dad and the pressure put on this poor handicapped boy."

So I told them about Wade's dad and his anger. I told them about the special ed aide who would rather gossip to Wade's dad than do her job. I told them about Benny, who stood up for Wade. Benny should be the hero of this whole mess and Wade, the victim. I was only the scapegoat. The cops let me go, but I was not allowed to go back to school for a week until this shooting thing blew over.

Hang Town

"Let's go hang downtown someday," said Shad, as we were yarding out a long hunk of tin off of a crumpled shed.

"In Sherwood?" I puffed.

"Naw, that's for lame junior high dorks!" yelled Shad. "Let's go into Portland on the Tri-Met. Ya got a board?"

I looked all around. All we had was boards. I grabbed one. "Like this one?"

Shad shook his head. "Naw, I mean like a longboard or at least a skateboard. Don't cha got a skateboard?"

I shrugged. "I used to have a board, but I sold it in Phoenix."

Shad put his hands on his hips. "Well, we gotta get you a board if we're going to hang in Portland. Let's go next Saturday."

I shook my head. "We can't go on a weekend. What about work? We might be starting to prune grapes again."

Shad was pounding nails, and he stopped and looked at me like I was a Martian from outer space. "Why the heck are you so gung ho about this stupid job? We don't even make minimum wage, and I've never even seen the old man ever give you any money."

"That's because I owe him big time. He bailed me out of jail," I said, as my ears turned red.

Shad beamed and took a sudden interest. "Sweet! Are you telling the truth? I mean I thought you were lying the other day. I didn't know you really had any serious jail bird in ya, Lyle. What were ya in for?"

"I took a minor over state lines and was busted for being a vagrant." I hung my head, embarrassed. Shad laughed, so I thought I'd better clear up my story. "It was only Benny. We ran away to Arizona."

"You and that nerd ran away?" Shad was hysterical. "Oh that is rich, Lyle, you should have taken Wade too!"

I grabbed Shad by the front of his coat with strength I didn't know I had. Shad's attitude really pissed me off.

"Don't you ever, EVER, laugh in any way at or about Benny and Wade again, Shad. You and I have some control over our lives—they don't, and I don't want to be your friend if you have that attitude." I choked him a little in his coat and let go.

"Okay, okay, Lyle," said Shad in a soft voice. "I'm sorry. You are right, it's just a strange story is all. I don't mean any disrespect. Well, think about hanging in Portland one day, won't cha? We will have a good time. I promise."

Planning for the
Portland Trip

Shad would have scoffed at me, but I don't care. If I'm really going to go somewhere, I now have a need to plan ahead. The trip will go better, and I will not get into too much trouble. I found out that there was a half day coming up at school. I looked at the Tri-Met schedule and realized that we would have to catch a bus halfway through second period in order to get to Portland at a decent time. I will insist on going to Powell's City of Books while we were there because I needed to get some books to pay off my library fine to Mrs. Bricks. Shad could appreciate the ditching of school for a period, and he would not need to know we were doing it so we would not have to wait for the next bus an hour after the time the final bell would ring. I had no trouble getting two field trip permit forms from the office when I lied that me and my buddy lost ours for the Biology Trip.

So on that Friday, we were all set with real field trip forms filled out and everything. My mom even gave me twenty dollars! Shad found an old skateboard that nobody wanted from the school lost and found, and we had warm hoodies and gloves and hats for the trip as every morning there was frost on the ground. I had English first period, and I asked Mr. Painter if he knew anything about building the new high school. "I don't live in Sherwood, Lyle, but I have not heard that information." He said. "Ask Mrs. Bricks. She's one of the few people I know among the staff who lives in Sherwood. She is the town historian and goes to all the city council meetings."

"Okay, I will, Mr. Painter," I said. I looked over at Janice. She looked really down. I wish that I would have asked her to come to Portland with me and Shad. I decided the next time we went, I would.

Adventure Into Portland

Most of the people that ride the Tri-Met bus are members of the invisible society that no one really wants to know about. There are the unemployed dads with their toddlers held tightly in their arms, the old Chinese man, the Indian woman, the hipster dude eating hummus, the haughty young babe, and the lady with the big voice who is telling the haughty babe from halfway across the bus that she's a bitch for sitting in a seat and not giving it to a little old lady with a shopping cart who can't stand upon the lurching bus.

Shad was used to riding the bus from the other side of Portland from Gresham. It was pretty confusing making the transfer at the transit center, so he was glad that I knew the way. Just last year at this time, our whole family had made our first trip from the train at Union Station and on to the bus all the way out to Sherwood. My mom and I, and sometimes the kids, had been in to Portland on the bus a few times after I got back from Arizona. We always went to Powell's Book Store.

Shad and I got off the bus in a whirl of people in back of Saint Mary's High School. There were cute girls everywhere, along with college students going up the street to Portland State and other people going down the street to city hall. Shad was dizzy looking at all the girls, and even more excited when we rounded the corner to the front of the school. We boarded around the block several times until a bell rang and the girls disappeared. Then we headed down the street to Pioneer Square. Now everything was quiet, and the sidewalks were pretty deserted. We could really go fast and do some jumps. I had not been on a skateboard for a longtime, but it didn't take long to get back into the groove.

As we got closer to the square, also known as Portland's living room, we could hear bells playing Christmas music.

Shad stopped. "Wow." He paused to listen. "That is actually beautiful. That is not cheesy Christmas music, even though it is the just about four days until Thanksgiving."

The echo of the bells on the tall buildings was fantastic as the last chimes ended with a long final note. The wind came up, and I shivered. "Man, at this time last year I was in Arizona, hanging out on the streets of Phoenix. We didn't even know which day was Thanksgiving, so we just made it up and ate a can of cold beans. I was in the slam for my birthday and on a train coming into Portland the day after Christmas."

We turned the corner to see the Square. There was a huge tree all lit up and garlands of green with giant red ribbons everywhere. It was overcast and dark. Down the street there was a swirling cloud of fog but no rain. There were all kinds of costumed dancers getting ready for a performance. In the middle was a huge dancing bear. We sat on the steps, mesmerized by the scene below.

Christmas Parade

After the show was over, everyone started down the street on the sidewalk. It wasn't a real parade, but everyone tagged along. We stayed at the end and cruised on our skateboards. The people ended up at a big mall called Pioneer Place. We went in to see a huge decorated tree that extended three stories. We rode the elevator all the way up to the top and down. We were just taking in all the sights when Shad saw some of his friends from Gresham. Shad marched over to these three guys and two girls. All of them, including Shad dressed in a uniform manner, long straight hair, ripped at the knee jeans, vests over heavy hoodies, big black boots, and wool hats that looked all the same.

Shad introduced everyone, and his buddy, Perry, took up the conversation. "Dude, let's all get high! We could go down to some park and take a huff!" Everyone was in favor of that, but no one moved.

So, Shad broke the silence. "So, yeah, then. Let's go down to the river!"

We all started out of the store and down to the Willamette River. Perry was leading the way. "So, Dude," he said turning to Shad. "What kind do ya got?"

Shad stopped dead in his tracks. "Kind? I don't have any weed, man."

"I thought you lived in Sherweed, man. Where's all the pot?" said Perry.

"I haven't seen any, man," said Shad.

"You mean you and this pip-squeak here aren't into, like, pounds of the weed?" asked Perry.

I decided to pipe up. "It's just a bunch of hype, Perry. The Sherwood kids made this "Sherweed" thing up so they would sound all tough and gangster. Most of the kids are just a bunch of preps."

"It's true," said Shad.

"Oh man!" shouted Perry. "Then we gotta go score some!" I took Shad aside. "It's getting late, Shad, and I need to get down to Burnside and Powell's. Do you know where the pizza place is across from Powell's? Why don't I meet you there in about two hours?"

Shad nodded. "Great idea, Lyle. That way, we do what we want, and you are not standing around all bored-like. I'll see ya at ..." He grabbed my wrist and looked at my watch. "At 4:00 p.m.!" Sure enough, when I got to the Pizza Place, Shad and his Gresham gang were feeding their faces.

Helping Hands

We got back to Sherwood pretty late because by the time we got on the streetcar and got back up to PSU, it was rush hour. The first bus came by and it was packed with people. I think only one girl got off, so we waited for the next bus. Luckily the buses were running every 15 minutes, but daylight disappeared by the time we got to Railroad Street in Sherwood.

"We're gonna have to walk to Brookman in the dark," I said.

"Well, maybe we can go up to Colfelt's Saloon and call on the landline. They let me do that once," said Shad. "It's worth a try. We could get Aunt Madge or your mom on the phone, and they could give us a ride."

"Maybe," I said, knowing how reluctant both of those women were to drive down to Sherwood this time of day.

But before we crossed the street, I could see this man in front of the Rebeckah's Hall having a problem juggling too many things in his arms. I ran over and caught a huge frozen turkey which had worked its way out of a soggy paper bag, before it crashed to the ground in a mud puddle.

"Good catch there, son," said the man. He was wearing the smallest, roundest, spectacles I had ever seen. He adjusted his funny spectacles and looked at me. "My name is Rich Ditto. Thank you."

"Do you need more help?" I asked as Shad poked a warning to shut up in my back.

"Sure!" said Rich. "My wife Dot is in there with the other folks from the Rotary. You can't miss her—she has glasses just like mine. They're packing Thanksgiving food boxes, and they all need to come out here to these cars. Then we will deliver."

"If we help, can we get a ride home?" asked Shad.

"Of course!" said Rich. "There's a rig going almost every where in and around Sherwood."

We went in, and there were all the Rotary people who helped me when I got beat up last year in the alley. The ones who remembered me slapped me on the back and said, "Hi, buddy." The tall one who took me home after they found me beat-up in the alley said, "Hey, man! Where have you been for all these months?"

"Oh, I took a trip to the Southwest," I spoke.

Well, we've got to get going," he said. "We all work together fast."

They had twelve tables full of boxes, and everyone had a frozen turkey in it. The rest of the people were filling each box with stuffing, green beans, cranberries, and other Thanksgiving food. All in one line, they efficiently filled bank after bank of boxes and folded the flaps.

"Take it away, boys!" said a Dot, who really looked just like Rich, right down to the glasses. We obeyed and took box after box out with a couple of other guys, and soon we had the van full. By that time, the line on the other side of the mass of tables was filled and so we took off our coats and started hustling again. After an hour, we were done with three vehicles we filled, ourselves.

"Now, you boys need a ride somewhere?" asked Rich.

"Yeah, we need a ride to Brookman Road and Middleton."

"Okay," said Rich. "Ride with Bill in the truck."

We jumped in the back of the truck with our boards. Bill made us get out of the back of the truck and climb in the cab because it's against Oregon law to ride in the back of a truck.

Shad sighed. "Oh man. Who the heck cares?"

"I care," said Bill, looking Shad straight in the eye.

"I guess you learn something new every day," joked Shad.

Bill was not in a joking mood. Before we got out of town, we delivered three boxes of food. We left Shad off at the beginning of the driveway at Madge's place, and after two more deliveries, Bill turned into our driveway.

"I can get off here," I said.

Bill looked at me. "Well, we still have to deliver the food." So Bill and I drove into the driveway got out the last of the food and came up to our door. I opened the door. Grandpa, Teddy, and Baby Mary were in the living room watching TV.

"Hi, guys!" I said as I walked to the kitchen with the heavy turkey box. Mom was coming out of the back room, and she gave me a look.

"Mom, come in the living room and meet Bill," I said as I pushed Mom ahead into the next room. Bill had a bag of potatoes and apple cider, which he handed over to Mom.

"Well, thank you, Bill," said Mom with a shocked look.

"Happy Thanksgiving," said Bill. "This is from Sherwood Helping Hands and the Evening Rotary."

Then Mom yelled over her shoulder, "Lyle, you are very late."

Having put down the box in the kitchen, I popped back in with a grin.

Bill spoke up, "Uh sorry, ma'am. We sort of hijacked your son and Madge's nephew to help us with the Thanksgiving Food Project."

"Well, thank you so much for the food," said my mom as she juggled the potatoes.

"No problem, Ma'am," said Bill as he tipped his baseball hat, turned, and left.

Oregon Bear

by Lyle Kent

Bear floated down Dairy Creek from the Coast Range Mountains. He found an old drift log and rolled it down the bank of the Tualatin River. Well, as you know, the Tualatin River means "slow moving," so it took two months for him to get down through the valley. Finally, he got tired and jumped off the log and onto a trail. The trail got bigger and bigger and soon, there was four lanes this way and four lanes that way with hard shiny horses zooming this way and that.

Well this is a strange place! He thought. *Where are all the other animals, and especially bears?* There were hard ribbon trails criss-crossing over and under each other. He got so dizzy looking at it that he fell off the track and ended up in a black field, which was filling up with the hard horses. It was raining snow, and he thought he would seek cover. He saw a huge square cave and decided to duck in. It looked like the general store that he sometimes used to see at Rose Lodge, only a lot bigger! Soon he saw a big picture of green and blue mountains and letters on wood like at the general store. The letters were R-E-I. He waddled into the cave within a cave and saw all kinds of things from the woods, trees, bushes, grass, and hiking boots. There were also tents and fake fires. There were fake rocks to scale everywhere. There were people all around but not many animals. A little boy and little girl ran up to him to pet his fur. That felt nice. So he licked the little girl. She tasted like honey! The girl and boy screamed and ran away.

In the middle of the store was a huge Doug Fir tree that towered overhead to a cliff. *Why lookie at all the pretty little stars shining through the limbs!* Marveled Bear. The tree was full of strange balls, and funny stuffed men in red suits, blue suits, and striped suits, and dollies, and bears, and red and white swirley canes. He climbed about halfway up the tree. He bit into some of the canes, but they didn't taste good so he threw them on the ground. That is when some men started yelling, "Hey, you, get down from there!" Women started screaming, and boys and girls were crying. Why are they so sad? Why are they so scared? This is such a nice tree. I can be the shining-bear star swinging up here in this tree!

He climbed up level with the cliff that had people on it, and they were yelling too. Then he saw a cliff on the other side with a big cougar standing there staring at him. He roared a greeting at him, but the cat just stared. Everyone else heard him because they roared back, screaming in their people voices. He jumped off the tree and on to the cat's cliff. The tree trembled with the shift of his weight but didn't fall over. The cat seemed friendly, so he took a nap right next to the cat. As he drifted off to sleep, Bear thought he could hear the cat purr.

Purrr! Purrr! Purr! Purrrrrrrrrrrrr! What a nice cat, thought Lyle. But then he woke up!

Striker, the house mouser, was snuggled next to me. Man, I need to quit having these folktale dreams, I thought to myself. I think I'm going crazy.

Honoring the Land

The next day was Thanksgiving, and so instead of thawing out a big batch of Fireman's Barbeque Chicken, Mom got up early and started on the turkey from Helping Hands. I was put in charge of the stuffing. It was really fun working with Mom all day in the kitchen. Grandpa and the kids watched the Portland Thanksgiving Parade, a couple of football games, played with toys, and caught a long catnap.

When at long last, with the kitchen in shambles and all the food on the table, we sat down to a feast. As soon as the eating slowed down, we started talking about the supposed new high school.

"No one knows about it, except for Mrs. Bricks," I said. "She went to a Washington County planning meeting, and they have a plan to add 30 to 50 thousand people to Sherwood in the next five years. That's why she thinks they need a second-high school."

Mom exploded, "That's just incredible! Where would they put all those people? And who will pay for all the new roads and services?"

"Us. The taxpayers," said grandpa softly.

"And who is going to benefit from this?" demanded Mom.

"Mrs. Bricks says there is going to be some vote on this. Did we get an election book in the mail?"

I asked as I went over to the table that holds all the mail these days.

The vote was to expand the urban growth boundary of the town by 130 acres. Grandpa took a look at the map and started laughing.

"Why, this is all the land near Cedar Creek that got flooded in '64 and '96! How do they plan to build houses on this?" Grandpa stabbed the map with his finger. "It's on the other side of Brookman Road from Madge's place."

"I wonder who owns all that property?" said Mom.

"It doesn't say on this," I said, handing her the booklet.

"Hmmm. It does say there is a hearing next Tuesday," said Mom.

"Sounds like a meeting the entire family should turn out for," I said, thinking of the entire "Kent Family Flash Mob" showing up. It really made me smile.

My mom slapped the election book on the table. "You know, this may seem petty, but I resent the fact that when I was in high school, kids would ask where I lived and I told them on this farm and they would say 'oh that's too bad that you are so poor.' Now I tell ladies at the store where I live, which is the exact same place and they say, 'oh you must be rich!' what a stupid world we live in."

"Ya wanna hear a funny song, Mama?" piped up Teddy.

Mom smiled. "Sure, Teddy!"

So he stood up and sang at the top of his voice:

"Row, Row, Row, your boat, gentle down the stream,
Merrily, merrily, merrily, life is but a dream!"

We all just smiled, but Teddy thought it was hilarious. "Get it, you guys? Life is a dream, like you are asleep. That's just silly!" Then he snickered some more.

The City Council Meeting

(Note: The following description of the City Council meeting is not verbatim. To see the exact transcript, go to www.citycouncilsherwood.org. The flag salute, introduction of councilors and guests, awards given to the Boy Scouts, and full names and addresses of those testifying are not included to avoid boredom.)

The place was swarming with people. We went in through the city side of the giant brick building, which was Sherwood's City Hall and Library. Mom and I knew that Madge was saving a chair for at least Mom and Grandpa. I wouldn't need a chair, since I was in charge of the Kent Family Flash Mob. The entire lobby into the chambers was full of people milling around, almost shoulder to shoulder. We cut through the people, sort of pushing our way through the standing throng. We could see Madge in the second row from the back holding her own and two more chairs and arguing with a very overweight lady about the chairs.

"I've got an old man and a sick lady with a baby who needs to sit here!" she shrieked at the lady. Luckily a man got up and offered his chair to the lady, and Grandpa and Mom slid into the saved seats. I stood at the end of the row by the window. Teddy was waving at some kids and a dog outside the window, so we were settled down for now.

The gavel came down and I looked up at the big wooden desk where the councilors sat. The "Gavel Banger" was none other than our friend Bill from Helping Hands! I had to look twice because he didn't have on his baseball cap and under his microphone it said: "Mayor Bill Smockwood."

"Mrs. Jane Bricks," said Mayor Bill. Mrs. Bricks, my librarian from the high school came forward to a table with a microphone before her and she started her speech.

"Pssst Psst" it was Teddy. He was pulling on my pant leg. He had a whole pad of sticky notes and he handed one up to me. It said "Hi Lyle! This is not pink!" I looked, and there by one of my feet on the floor was Janice! I sank down on the floor. "Janice! Hi! What are you doing here?" I probably sounded pretty dopey.

She whispered, "We live on the land that they are going to develop. They are going to kick us off before the end of the year if this vote passes."

"Oh, man, Janice. I'm so sorry," I whispered. Above, the crowd was humming and Mrs. Bricks was presenting facts and figures about a budget deficit.

Janice continued, "We have 35 head of Nubian Goats. I don't know what we are going to do with them if we have to leave." said Janice.

Suddenly, the crowd went wild with applause and whistling.

"Quiet down, quiet down" said Mayor Bill as he banged the gavel "This is a hearing, so let's hear, only, please!"

Mrs. Bricks continued, "There are plans that are so far reaching, they defy sanity. Do you people out there realize that there is a plan to add 30 to 50 thousand people to this town in five years?" People just looked at each other stunned. "We do not even have the sewage capacity for that kind of population. So, in conclusion, I would just like to say that moral courage is needed in our world today. We need to make right decisions; not your decision, not my decision... (The bell rang saying her time was up, but Mrs. Bricks kept on talking.) Decisions, which are not just for you or for me, but are about and for our community!"

The entire room, except for the first two rows of people who were lawyers, developers, and land owners, started cheering. All the people in the lobby, and all the people outside the windows were standing up, cheering, and clapping. Mrs. Bricks stood up, gathered her papers, and walked to the side of the room.

"We will take a three-minute break!" said Mayor Bill over the cheering as he pounded on the big desk.

Teddy crawled his way down the row of chairs to check in with Mom. Milly and Billy were sitting with Madge, but as soon as they saw Teddy, they all got antsy and started crawling through the legs of the people to the other side of the room. I started picking up the post-it notes that Janice had given Teddy that were now scattered all over the floor. Janice had moved over to talk to a lady and man who I assumed were her parents.

Soon everyone was called back to order, and the men who spoke next were the two "stuffed suits" as Grandpa called them. The one who used to be the mayor last year spoke:

"I own the eastern section of the land in question," he said, "I pay my taxes on this land, and I have also served as your mayor for four years." (He paused for some applause, but there was just a polite slapping.) "I think as a loyal taxpaying American, I deserve property rights as well as the next person. I can do anything I want with my land. I want to build our community, not tear it down by leaving all sorts of farm trash all over. We could have another beautiful development for our city. Our "Brookman Addition" will have 256 houses and two four-story low-income apartment complexes. With another development, we will add to the low-income housing offerings for the workforce of the new Walmart Superstore." (He paused again for some clapping, but a couple of old farmers who live on Brookman Road started booing. At the same time, the anti-Walmart people started chanting "No Walmart No Walmart" and waving their signs.)

The gavel went down several times. "Order! Order," yelled Mayor Bill. "I want to remind everyone that this is a hearing, and everyone will have their say. Do you have something to say, James?" This was the other look-alike brother.

"Yes, I do, Mister Mayor. As you know," chimed in the other stuffed shirt, "Our county has a master plan underway to add several thousand more people into our community. We are also proposing a second-high school for our community. These will be big changes to boost our economy."

People in the audience were sort of confused about these statements about a sudden need for a new high school, so there was some talking among themselves.

"Here." said the first stuffed shirt. "Let me show you some figures. We have taken the time to make a graphic."

The other stuffed shirt stepped five paces over to a chart pack. When he moved it, he exposed three little terrorists—Teddy, Milly, and Billy who had not only drawn a large turkey over the entire page of numbers but had also painted their faces with the ink pens! Everyone pealed with laughter. I dove across the room and corralled the kids back over by the window. Mayor Bill banged his gavel, and people began to chuckle and chat to each other again. The anti-Walmart people started in again: "NO WALMART! NO WALMART!"

"ORDER!" shouted Mayor Bill. Finally, everyone was quiet.

"Uh well," said stuffed shirt number one. "The numbers are impressive, and I can get you councilors a printout of this plan."

"Councilors," said Mayor Bill. "Are there any questions?"

The blonde-haired lady councilor spoke up, "I was not at the last County Commissioner meeting. Is this what they talked about? Population expansion? I thought it was going to be on road improvement."

Stuffed shirt number one said, "Well, yes we er, I, er, they, talked on a number of items. The road improvement, the expansion of the UGB, and the new Sherwood Town Center plan."

"Oh, are they finally going to plan to do something in Old Town?" asked the councilor with the glasses.

"No, the NEW town center!" said stuffed shirt two. The bell rang, and the audience started talking to each other, and I hustled the kids to the side of the room.

"Uh, next up is Mr. Peacock," said Mayor Bill. This man strutted over, just like a bird.

"Good evening, Mr. Mayor and Council. I am Mr. Charles Peacock from the Geologist consulting group, Williams, Hardtack, and Peacock to go over the significant ramifications of this UGB extension. Our little history today is the story of the building up and tearing down of the land. Fifteen thousand years ago, the land that we know of as Sherwood, Oregon, USA was covered by the Missoula Floods. This was a building process of a high plain due to the flooding alluvial into our area. The land on the opposite bank of Cedar Creek had laid fallow for thousands of years, and now is the best time to build it up. It is a perfect woodland of ash and alders. It will make a wonderful new rural development."

"That all you got?" said Mayor Bill.

"Yep," said Mr. Peacock.

"Okay," sighed Mayor Bill. "Mr. Lowe is next." There was a murmur in the crowd as my great-grandfather got up from his chair and hobbled up to the table. The crowd murmured in amazement, "Oh, my gosh! It's crazy old man Lowe. He's a looney. Well, he's an old man. He will tell them a thing or two. But he's crazy! What could he possibly know about urban planning?"

Grandpa drew the microphone up to his mouth. "I would specifically like to address the annexation of this Urban Growth Boundary and the development there on Brookman Road," he said, as he waved the election booklet in the air. "Mr. Peacock is right. The Missoula Floods did come through our countryside here, and it laid down a very thick layer of alluvial rock and soil, which is unstable during earthquakes and flooding. You might wonder what happens to the gravel in your driveway over the years, it sinks. So does your concrete over time, it cracks, and breaks, and could sink, if we lived long enough to see it. I have seen this place where you want to plant these houses for over the last eighty years. It is sort of a strange swamp land covered with water-loving trees. It is like a sponge and part of the Cedar Creek waterway.

In 1962, the Columbus Day Storm blew down half of the trees. The ground was so wet there that no one could haul out those trees, even in the summer. Old Mr. Brookman couldn't get down the logging road more than fifty feet. So, in 1964, we had a hundred-years flood, mostly because of snow melt. Keith Sterns and I got his motor boat down there and started pulling those logs in the water. I got them up on a bit of high ground and bucked them up. I still was doing it after the big flood of '69, and the worst flood of that land was in 1996–why, it went right up to the road, then flooded the whole road out for a quarter of a mile. There are many low flood places right on Railroad Street, Oregon Street, and even Willamette Street. That part of downtown has been covered with water.

So you got a floodplain there in your Brookman Addition, and you can't plant houses on a floodplain. You also would be destroying a natural feature of a wet land, which protects the flooding downstream.

"I also object to the idea that the land is fallow. Fallow means the land is useless, but that is not true of that land. The land has already proved useful in a natural way. Some of my neighbors also tell me that there is a small Nubian Goat ranch started on one of the parcels. Another farmer sells eggs. Across the road, there are many farms trying to produce things for the farmer's markets..." The bell rang and Grandpa stood up and walked back to his chair. No one said anything. He totally made sense.

"Madge Brookman and Gail Kent," announced Mayor Bill. Madge and Mom stomped up front to the table with the microphone. Teddy, Billy, and Milly stomped up there too, and I realized for the first time that this was their library story time room, so they felt like this was their place. Those kids owned this room. They lined up in front of their Moms at the table, like they were going to be entertained and sat on their butts. I knew they were going to stay put for a while.

Madge spoke first, whipping out a newspaper. "Mister Mayor, it was only last month that you said in the newspaper, and I quote: 'I am worried about the City Budget and I think we need to go over it again and see if we can cut some more money.' But then just a week later there is talk of expanding more shopping centers, adding on to the Urban Growth Boundary of our town, and building a new high school. Considering all the city services required for all of this, you think we, as taxpayers, or that the city can afford it, especially with our poor economy right now?"

Mayor Bill grabbed the microphone and said: "No, I do not think we can afford it."

"So," said Madge. "Without any notification or discussion with the community, you are proposing to spend more money when you know we cannot afford the budget we have now?

Oddly enough, Mayor Bill was pleased with this allegation, although it seemed quite damaging. He chuckled: "No. I am not proposing to do something that we cannot afford. That is why I question the status of our city budget," said Mayor Bill. "Would anyone else on the board care to weigh in on this?"

Looking from left to right each member said, "No, I recuse myself, No, No." The fifth one said, "We have been talking about this UGB expansion for three years now. If I recall, the last time we put it to a vote last fall, it was voted down. Now we are simply bringing it up again." There was silence.

Mayor Bill turned to Madge and Mom. "The clock is on. Do you have anything more to say?"

Mom grabbed the mic. "Yes, if every election costs money to run, and the Urban Growth Measure was voted down last year, why would the city 'simply bring it up again'? Isn't that a waste of money?" The audience murmured over this, but Mom went back to her written speech: "Every year we asphalt and concrete more and more land. There is a thing in Arizona called 'Heat Islands'–hardened off land covered with cities. They are 50 percent as hot as natural areas. Here in Oregon, soon there will be no more natural areas to absorb all the rain. How will the wells in Sherwood do then? What sort of future will our children have when we kill off every form of nature?" People sort of nodded at each other in the audience and the bell rang.

"Thank you, ladies. Uh, Mr. Ray Reinke and Esmeralda, uh, Reinke?" announced Mayor Bill. Nothing happened, and Madge and Mom looked back before they got up. Their eyes opened wide with surprise when they saw the commotion out in the lobby. The Police Chief who was at one of the lower tables turned to the door and held his hand over his gun.

Two bells rang, and neither one was the city council bell. A low voice announced, "Make way! Make way, let a lady through!" The bells rang wildly, and in strode a mountain of a man with a huge plaid farm coat and a leather hat with ear flaps that were fluttering up and down to the rhythm of his bouncing footsteps. He wore rubber boots, covered with mud. Following him was a long, tall, cowboy, in muddy cowboy boots, jeans, and a leather vest. He was pulling a dairy cow, on a long pink satin ribbon. She minced along, twisting this way and that and holding a striped Victoria's Secret shopping bag and a cow bell. "Make way, make way... for Miss Esmeralda..." said Mr. Ray as the entire packed crowd in the chambers crammed together to let this huge man, cowboy, and cow by.

"That's Esmeralda the Christmas Cow!" yelled one of the little girls. Teddy, Billy, and Milly were jumping up and down, clapping and shrieking. For them it was the best story time ever. Being a parade cow, it was Esmeralda's cue to start lightly flinging candies into the crowd. People forgot why they were there and started diving for the candy. Mr. Ray Reinke picked up the candy on the floor and handed it out to the little ones.

"ORDER!" roared Mayor Bill. He turned to the bigman and cow who were now at the desk with the microphone. The cowboy stood by to rein in the cow. "Mr. Reinke—you'd better have something good to say."

Mr. Ray Reinke grabbed the mic to speak. The cow sat down in the other chair and crossed her legs. She had on rubber boots with damp mud and other barnyard material on them. The floor was filthy. Mr. Reinke drew up his breath and began to speak:

"Mayor Bill and City Council, we represent the agricultural community of this town. There was a day when all corners of our countryside was flowing with onions, strawberries, apples, cherries, beans, and wheat." Esmeralda rang her cowbell. Ray jumped. "Oh and dairy! Agriculture was Sherwood's biggest industry. Our little town was an agricultural center with an active cannery and banks and stores supporting the farmer. Nowadays, more and more people have come to our little place in the world to live in a bucolic setting with a small-town feel. If we get rid of every small farm and harden every inch of virgin land with cement and asphalt, there will be nothing left for people to come here for. They come for the rural atmosphere and small-town feeling. But instead, it will look like every other urban sprawl-development in the nation. We must think of what we are doing, for the future!" As Ray said this, he pointed to the little kids who were mesmerized on the carpet. There was a huge cheer through the whole chamber. The cow jumped up from her chair and was loudly ringing her bell to encourage the audience. The cowboy yanked on the pink satin ribbon, and the cow started moving out with Ray and the cowboy. The anti-Walmart people started chanting and flashing their signs in the air.

Ray moved to squeeze out through the cheering crowd again as Mayor Bill banged his gavel. "We will now have a ten-minute recess," he hollered.

Back at School

We didn't get home until midnight. The meeting went on and on. After Mr. Ray and the cow got up there, everyone wanted to speak. Who knows, if anyone changed anybody's mind. I was nodding off in my scrambled eggs in the cafeteria the next day at school when I was pounded on the back by Shad.

"Dude! I heard all about the big meeting last night! Man, you guys rocked!" he shouted.

I looked at him bleary-eyed. "Oh yeah? Where were you last night? How come you weren't there for some anarchy?"

"That's because I got some freedom from the 'fam'. I could do what I wanted, and I smoked a little weed without having to go outside and freeze my butt. Who wants to waste time fussing over some development? They're gonna win in the end." Shad walked away triumphant.

I stuffed my mouth and took off for English class. Janice was already sitting in her seat by the window. How am I going to approach her?

"Uh, so you have–what kind of goats?" Well, that was pretty lame.

She turned and looked at me. "They are registered Nubians. They are all white, and one of the biggest kind of goat. They are milking goats. We supply milk for people that have digestion problems. We used to live way into the coast range from up Highway 34 near Five Rivers, but the man who owned the land decided to log it so we had to move. Now my dad is either going to sell the goats or find a new place—whatever comes first. He has ads in the paper for both. I used to go to school on Star Schools on the Internet—"

"So did I!" I broke in. "Last year!"

"Really?" she said.

Then the bell rang, and Mr. Painter started class. "Okay, everyone, so how did you like the story about the salmon?"

"It was stupid," said one of the football guys sitting nearest to the door.

Mr. Painter stared at the guy. "And why do you think it was stupid?"

"Because kids do not fall in the river and become salmon." The burly football guy rolled his eyes. "Then the salmon talks to the Indian and the seal about what he does. It's dumb. These are baby stories."

"Well," Mr. Painter countered. "They are ancient Native American stories, and they are a form of folklore that has served its purpose, low these many millennium. You probably read Tall Tales when you were little. Ones like Paul Bunyan or Pecos Bill. These Native American legends are a bit more sophisticated." Mr. Painter turned toward the windows. "So tell me, Lyle, what do you think these silly stories are used for?"

Mr. Painter had never called on me before, and I had not talked in class, so it took me a second to find my voice.

"Ah, well these are ancient stories from the Native Americans. They were told when there were no scientific studies of the salmon and their migration, and so I think that the people were making up a story to explain what was going on in nature."

"So these people were making sense of their world," said Mr. Painter. "I think before we read our next novel, Their Eyes Were Watching God by Nola Neal Hurston, we should try our hand at writing a story like that." The boys in the back started to groan. Mr. Painter was not going to give up—he never gave up.

"Janice—what stories do you know that explain natural or scientific things?" At first, I thought Janice was going to get up and leave, but she didn't. She had an answer.

"There is a metaphorical love story about–I think it was Mount Rainer and Mount Hood fighting over Mount Saint Helens. It started with two "boy mountains," who were, at first humans from two tribes, bragging and fighting over the girl. The boy from the Multnomah tribe was turned into a mountain. I guess he became Mount Hood, and he got mad and blew his top. This is how they saw the volcanic eruption. The other boy and girl were also turned into mountains: Mount Rainer and Mount Saint Helens. It was another Native American story, and I think many of the early pioneers heard that story, and they repeated it, even though the scientific world knew about volcanoes during the days of the white settlers."

Mr. Painter was now on a roll. "Okay, so let's make a list of ideas that we could base a story on in metaphorical terms." Mr. Painter turned to the white board and students started yelling out ideas.

Tornados!	The birth of the earth	Football
playoffs!	Butterflies!	Birth of stars
Hurricanes	Bird migration	Cancer
Earthquakes	Grasshoppers	Ghosts
	Werewolves	

Election Results

Wednesday morning, the radio was blaring in the kitchen, and everyone was eating breakfast. Suddenly the newsman announced:

"And in the Sherwood Annexation issue, the vote for an enlarged Urban Growth Boundary won by a narrow, one percent margin. This is the third time in two and a half years that the initiative has been up to the voters, and it has passed."

"No!" yelled Mom.
"I don't believe it!" I said.
"It was just a matter of time that they would wear us down," said Grandpa bitterly.
"Boooooo!" yelled Teddy and Baby Mary.
What was going to happen to Janice's family and the goats?

Up to Thinking Rock

I've been up here many times, now that I know a better route to take. I walk up La Brousse Road to the end—although it is not the end anymore because there is this steep road that goes up to a housing development. It is a gated community with a big iron gate that swings open with a plastic card key. I have noticed there are cracks in the asphalt and it looks like it is slowly sliding downhill, just like Grandpa described at the City Council meeting. By the time I die, if they don't fix it, it will slide right down the hill. Fat chance.

Anyway, the day is December 16—my birthday, and it is clear and cold. I am now sixteen years old. Mom said I could do whatever I wanted to do today, so I decided it was time to take Teddy up to my thinking spot that overlooks the valley. I bundled him up and told him we were going on an adventure.

"Oh. Are we going to the North Pole and see Santa?" he asks.

"No not today. We are going to my secret place called Thinking Rock," I told him.

He jumped through the front door. "Wow! That sounds like lots of fun!"

He chattered all the way up the hill about some game that he thinks he is going to get for Christmas.

It is some wild video game called Land Skyler for Xbox. I knew he's not going to get it because it costed over a hundred dollars, and my mom was not going to spend a hundred dollars on anyone in the family. I figured Teddy had a right to fantasize about this game for now.

"You are the warrior, and you have the gold an' a weapon... Den, BLAST! You kill all the monsters at the end of the game!" he said.

By now we were starting up the steep part of the hill. Teddy was huffing and puffing because he doesn't get enough exercise. I stopped so Teddy could catch his breath and pointed up the tree-lined top of the ridge with its saw blade zigzag shape. "When it starts to snow, we will go clear to the top and get some sleds or garbage can lids and come down this hill."

Teddy's eyes bugged out. "Wow! Oh! Look how high up we are!"

We are only halfway up the hill, but after another twenty feet, we turned off the road, and I opened up the limbs of a small tree, and we stepped onto a trail. We climbed up a ridge, then went down into a deep creek bed, came up the other side, and then we climbed again. We got up to a flat space, and Teddy stopped for a bit.

"All we have to do now is climb around those rocks and we will be on top." I explained.

When we got around on the other side of the bluff, we were higher than ever before, and we could see clear to Highway 99. We could see part of Grandpa's vineyard.

Chehalem Mountain was looming out of a ground fog bank, and the shiny ribbon of Chapman Road reflected in the mist. In back of us, all we could see was a large forested area where dark Parrett Mountain rose up like a wall. Finally, to the northwest, we could see the strange alder and ash grove where Janice and her family lived. Since the trees had lost their leaves, I could actually see her house and barn. In another year, it would be just another sea of house roofs.

"So what do we do now?" asked Teddy, after we exhausted all the sights.

"Well, usually I think, Teddy. But, today, I have to come up with a story for my English class," I said.

Teddy looked like he was ready to settle down on a rock couch to hear it. "Okay. What is it about?"

Dark Raven and the New Ocean

by Lyle Kent

I am Dark Raven. I was once a child who lived on the Big River. But one day, I fell in the Big River and would have gone to live with the Salmon People if it wasn't for another raven who swooped me out of the river and changed me into a raven too.

I learned to fly long distances and see the world way past Big River to the Rock Mountains and all the way west to the ocean. The ocean was bigger than the river or any of the Klamath Lakes, and it always roared. I could fly over all the mountains or land in the lowest river marsh. I would bring the news of the land to all the animals and people.

One day, I was sitting on that mountain right over there. They now call it Wild Horse Mountain, but long ago it had no name and was not as tall.

I was sunning my dark green, iridescent wings in the morning sun, looking to the east, perched on the tallest Doug Fir around. Then, I heard a rumbling. I looked to see if the mountain I was on was moving, but the sound came from the east. It sounded like the ocean roaring. I flew toward the sound and got to the place where Big River and Long South River came together. The water was swelling, then churning, then rumbling with large rolling boulders. There were floating chunks of ice, looking like ferry boats, carrying pink and gray chunks of granite on them. This scene was most curious. There had been no big rains in months. Where was all this water coming from?

I saw a human running from the water, and I swooped down and carried him to the top of a steep ridge. He was yelling thanks, but I could see that there were many people and animals being swept by the water. Some were washed right up to the ridge, and they clambered onto the rocks and trees as fast as they could go to get higher on the mountain. I looked for humans in trees, bears on rocks, and deer on hillocks and tried to fly them to safety. Finally, I was back to the mountain where I began and tried to warn the animals there. Some ran up the mountains where the natives lived in the summer. I swooped up as many humans and animals as I could. Soon, the water filled the deep creek beds, and then–*swoosh!* A tide of water, rocks, and ice chunks with boulders, all flooded the ground. Just as I thought, the water would go over the lip-ridge of the mountain and over into the deep valley, there was a slop! My big mountain grew up like a big human hand. It rose up from the ground to stop the water. Large waves of water roared, and the earth shook. The water bounced back away from the mountain and streamed back the way it came!

I was so tired; I flew up to my big Doug Fir to watch the most amazing thing! To the North and East, I could see all that water swirling, in five or six whirlpools going around and around. Some of the animals shouted, "It is over! It is over!"

I crowed, "No! No! Do not go down! Stay up here! Stay up here!" Most of the animals did stay, but some were foolhardy and curious and raced down to the muddy, rocky land below. They were caught in the mighty whirlpools with huge trees that were stirring the mud into a chocolate pudding. The valley to the east was a sea of water. Only the great white-headed mountains who were lovers of long ago held their heads above the flood.

The next morning, there was another swoop of water barreling toward the mountain ridge. It was not as deep as the first, but the land was changed in one day from deep valleys cut by babbling creeks to wide-open muddy plains, filled with a deep layer of rocks and mud. Over on the other side of the mountain, there was not as much water, but the Long South River that swung around the mountain was flooded for a very long time.

The humans on the south side of the mountain were saved from the flood. I guided the humans who survived on the north to the other side of the mountain. The humans had to be helped because they are not as sturdy as the animals, but at the same time, they make songs and dances that no animal can do. None of us will never know why the ocean of water came from the east, and we hope the ocean of the west will say its banks. It was a curious event.

"Wow!" exclaimed Teddy. "That's a great story, Lyle. You could make that into a video game!"

"Yeah. It has potential. But I'd rather just get it written up for English and turn it in," I said as we walked back down the hill.

Christmas Signs

This year, our family was really in the holiday spirit. I know that I was pretty stoked ever since Shad and I went to Portland. I wanted this Christmas to be special, but how? I wanted to give great gifts, sing songs, and tell Christmas stories. One day, Grandpa and I went over to the neighbors who bought our barn wood. They were in their cozy workshop with a woodstove with benches covered with boards to paint. They showed me how to letter a sign and how to paint a protective coat of shellac over the painting. I went outside and cleaned up a bunch of old boards, dried them out, and cut them into sign shapes. Over the few days I had until Christmas, I made these signs:

Teddy Bear Junction—for Teddy
Gone Fish'in—for Grandpa
Genius at Work—for Baby Mary
Get out of My Kitchen!!!—for Mom
No Snivel'in—for Madge
I Hate Pink!—for Janice
I Live in Sherweed!!!—for Shad

Grandpa's New (Old) Friend

I can't believe the good luck it was when Grandpa started to visit Toon Waldo. He lived out at the old-folks home at Avamere near what Grandpa called 6-corners (even though there were only 4 corners now because they aligned two main roads together and put a stoplight there). I guess when my mom went to high school, three roads came together—one being the four lane split highway 99W, and there was no stoplight at all. Mom says the kids on the bus would just shut their eyes as the bus driver would barrel across the intersection every time he thought the road was clear!

Grandpa phoned "Old Toon"—that's what everyone called him—and they talked a long time. They set up a time to visit on Fridays from about 2 in the afternoon until 6 when Toon would go get his dinner. They played cards and chess. I would get to hang out at the school on Fridays, and then go meet up with them and get a ride home.

Three weeks after Christmas, Mom lost her job at the Home Depot and started babysitting Millie and Billy while Madge got on as a cashier at Target. People in town teased Madge and Mom about selling out to the Big Box when they so opposed the Walmart, but somehow people still had to pay bills and put food on the table. I asked grandpa about this and he said, "Darned if you do and darned if you don't." I totally knew what he really meant.

I was now 16 and my mom started staring at me in a funny way like she used to at Dad. I thought that she probably missed him, and maybe I reminded her of him. It was still very hard to think about my dad dying in Afghanistan—a half a world away from us.

One day as we were waiting for grandpa to squeeze in the car with the chattering toddlers, my mom gave me that look, and then she spoke, "I think you should start driving, Lyle."

I was flabbergasted. "You mean like driving this car?"

"Yes," she said softly. "From now on, we will start practice driving on Sunday, and we will go over right now and get a driver's manual." And believe it or not, that is exactly what we did.

Land Over Time

January, February, March, April...time flowed on through the calendar in the dining room. The land remained the same–bare trees, fog, rain, wind. The vegetation kept on disintegrating as we pruned the vineyard and stacked the used lumber. I finally paid off my debt to grandpa, and now I was making minimum wage. I got a bank account to save money. Mom put me on her auto insurance, and I had to pay for that. Just after spring break, my mom found a day to take off from the rug rats, and I didn't have to go to school so we could go to the DMV to take my driving test. We spent most of the day waiting and going through the process and–I got my license! My nerves were shot by the whole ordeal, and then my mom made me drive to the Yogurt Bear for a celebration, and then home. "Now," my mom informed me, "If the gas tank is down to a quarter, it is up to you to fill it before you come home." More expense.

All this time went by and the anti-Walmart people had raised money to pay lawyers to take their case to the State of Oregon. The people pushing for the new high school were silent, and no one had kicked Janice and her family off of the goat farm. It seemed like the land was winning the battle to stay just the way it has always been.

I got to drive the car to school on Fridays. There was a deal worked out that when Madge went to work at 4:00 p.m. in the afternoon, she would take grandpa to the Old Folks place to see Toon Waldo. They had dinner together these days, and I was supposed to pick up grandpa at 8:00 p.m. That way I got to hang out at school and go to the first half of the basketball games.

Then things got complicated. At the end of April, we had the month "go out like a lion" as grandpa told everyone. I had a feeling on that Friday that there was a real storm coming in. It made me nervous because I had to drive. I grabbed my yellow raincoat off the hook and put it on. I got in the car with the wind blowing sideways and the rain drenching everything in large wet slaps. There was a rhythm to it: Woo, Woo, Woo, Slap, slap, slap. Woo, Woo, Woo, Slap, slap, slap… The wind was wheezing like a locomotive. My windshield wipers could not keep the drenching rain from obscuring my vision. I crept out of the driveway and onto the road and decided not to go the way of the highway but through the back way on Brookman Road.

When I started up Brookman, I squinted to see a small shadow—no, maybe two small shadows— one with an inside-out umbrella, hunched halfway down to the side of the road! It was Janice and her six-year old brother, Arlo. I pulled over in a wide spot and told them to get in the car. They stood outside and said they would wait for the bus. They looked just pitiful.

"No," I commanded through the gusting rain. "You guys get in the back of the car—even fora few minutes. You guys need to get out of this storm." So they got in. We waited for the bus for five minutes, and it did not come. "Look, Janice, I can take you and your little brother to school. I've got a license and everything. You'll have to take the bus home because I have to stay in town and pick up Grandpa this evening."

"We can't just get in a car and drive off without our parent's approval," said Janice.

Naturally, she was right. "Okay, I'm much dryer than you guys, so I'll go and talk to your folks. If the bus comes by, get on it and if not, I'll take you to school."

I questioned this plan after the first fifty yards down the driveway. There were huge potholes merging into a lake right in the middle of the lane. On the other side of this brown lake, I could see someone in a yellow slicker just like mine but with matching yellow pants. It was Janice's dad. I waved at him, and he waved back and got within earshot. I told him about the bus and that the kids were in my car. He yelled thanks and told me it was okay if I took them into town. So then I slogged back to the car. On the way back, another dip in the drive was filling with water. I tried to go around it, and I slipped into the muck. All this time the wind and rain kept up wheezing and drenching.

I got back in the car. The bus still had not come by, so we started down the road, but when we approached the intersection of Brookman and the bottom of Ladd Hill Road, we could see red and blue flashing lights through the bare trees. Then we saw flares and a guy in a slicker.

"The road is closed up ahead," he yelled. "I'm going to have to get you to turn around and use 99W."

So with much effort, we turned around the narrow margins of the road. I started to spin in the mud, but the slicker man shoved on the back of the car, and we bounced free from that mud-sucking ditch. Then we went back the same way we came. When we got to Janice's place, there were six goats standing by the side of the road. "Those goats are pretty smart. They know the place is flooding," I said too casually.

"Flooding!" screamed Janice and Arlo at once from the backseat. Before I could say anything, there was Janice's dad.

"What happened?" he asked as he stood by my rolled down window.

"The road at Ladd Hill is blocked, so we had to turn around," I said. "We are going to take 99W. When I get to school, I'll call Madge, and she can help you get these goats out of the road. She has a truck, and she can take them up to her place or down to ours. It looks like we are going to see Grandpa's 100-year flood."

"Yeah," said Janice's dad. "It's bad karma. Your grandpa was right."

Suddenly three more goats scrambled up onto the road.

"Okay," said Janice's distracted dad. "You kids get to school."

We got Arlo to Hopkins School and took him to the office. He was shivering to death, with his teeth chattering. They took him to the school nurse, and she got him some spare clothes and told us he would be okay. We went on to school and changed into our PE clothes. We took our coats and wet clothes to Mrs. Bricks in the library to dry, but she took one look at the muddy clothes and said she would take them to home economics. and wash them. She gave me a spare denim jacket and Janice her library sweater. I called Madge on Mrs. Brick's phone.

Hippies in the Living Room

Our place was a mess when I got Grandpa home. Janice and her family were sleeping on our living room floor. All the kids were bouncing on some borrowed mattresses. When Orin and Violet, Janice's folks, left the farm, there was six inches of water in the back end of the house where the kitchen was. They got the goats rounded up that escaped to the road. Then Orin had to had to call Madge later because the entire barn was full of water, so all of the goats were herded through the swampy land, onto the road, and into the truck. They were now all up at Madge's place.

Janice's folks were pretty interesting. Here they were sitting on mattresses with tie dye T-shirts and pajamas. I didn't really realize that they were Hippies. Janice and Arlo didn't dress like Hippies, but Orin and Violet were in some sort of tie dye all the time. They were the first Hippies I had ever really paid attention to. Janice was really defensive.

"Okay, okay. My mom and dad are probably the youngest hippies in Oregon. They went to University of Oregon in Eugene. I think that my mom's parents lived on a commune when they were first married. Just don't say anything at school, okay, Lyle?"

"Oh, I won't," I promised. "But why are you so angry about it?"

"I got teased about it when my parents came to school," she said. "I got in a big fight with some girls, and I got kicked out of Waldport Junior High. That's why I had to do Star School."

It rained all night, and the next day, but slowed down to a steady drizzle by Sunday morning. After lunch, it was almost clear and we all hiked down to the goat farm to check the damage. The giant puddle-lakes were everywhere, linking into each other. Grandpa and Orin borrowed the sign painter guy's truck and hauled the aluminum boat down to the farm where they unloaded it into the swampy alder grove. We floated and guided the boat with poles of alder limbs along to the house. The family car was up to its hubcaps in water, and the front porch had water up to the first step. We tracked into the house. The front room was dry, but the dining room and kitchen drooped toward the back and water was standing two and three inches deep. Out the window of the kitchen, the water covered the yard and looked like there was a current running through it.

We looked for things that people needed like clothes, food, and medicine. We gathered it in bags and boxes, filled the boat with everything, and guided it back out to the road. Things were light enough that we were able to get the boat with all the loaded stuff back into the truck and back down to our house.

By Thursday, the flood went down, and Janice's family slowly moved back into the house. By the next Friday, all the goats were moved, but Orin had to buy a load of hay because the grass and shrubs were covered with mud.

In Deep Weeds

After the rain, the sun came out everyday and it got pretty warm. Then the grass and weeds burst out of the ground. Grandpa noticed that the grapes were being smothered, and so all hands were on deck to hoe weeds and cut grass. Shad was hired on to hoe, much to his disgust. "I tell you if these weeds were real weed, you guys would be rich!" His snide comments did not help.

Shad didn't show up for work on Sunday, so Grandpa and I were out there by ourselves, pulling weeds around the grapes, cutting the grass, and raking it up. We took turns doing each job over time so that Grandpa would not get, as he said, "Stove-up." (Whatever that meant.)

"Next Friday, when you come to pick me up, Lyle, I want you to come in and meet Old Toon." said Grandpa.

"Now when you first meet him, he's gonna say, 'Play me a game of chess.' If you don't want to play him, you should say, 'Sure I'll play you, but you will beat me.' Then he won't want to play."

I nodded as I pulled out a big pigweed. "Sure, grandpa. I'd like to meet him. Why does everyone call him, Toon?"

"Because he used to work for Disney, and he drew cartoons," said grandpa.

I looked up at grandpa. "Oh Wow! That's pretty cool. I'd like to write screenplays someday."

Grandpa looked straight at me. "Really? That's hard work—to tell the truth. It takes a lot of imagination to see the truth. But the wilder your imagination, the less surprised you are about what's really going on."

I started cutting the grass. "Well, all I know is that writing is something I'm good at. I have to believe in something I'm good at, so I'm sticking with it."

Grandpa's eyes got wild like they did the first day we met him, before he started taking his medication. "I'm going to tell you a secret, but I don't want you to go blabbing it to anyone—not your mom, or Janice, or Teddy or any of your friends at school. No one can know this. Those anti-Walmart people have been doing some investigation since the flood, and something's going to happen. I don't know what, but it's going to happen! Do you believe me?"

I was a bit unnerved, but I shook my head up and down. "Yep, Grandpa, I believe you, and actually, I am not surprised."

When You Least Expect It

It was the last day of May. All week, there had been flocks of fourth graders parading around town re-enacting the Pioneer Days. Everyone dressed like pioneers and pulled homemade wagons. I had fun running into these kids before and after school. They would be slouched around on park benches, moaning and groaning about walking from their school to the History Museum and back. They were amusing, and I laughed at them behind their backs.

I didn't like riding the bus, so I always walked to school, except for Fridays. After the flood I was allowed to drive Janice and Arlo to school every Friday. Then, after school I'd hang out and catch a few softball or baseball games. At 8:00, I go pick up Grandpa, which meant I'd have to park and go in and get him and see Toon.

Toon was beating Grandpa at chess when I got there, but Grandpa rallied with a check. Toon's eyes were shining when he saw me. "So how's your girlfriend's family doing with the goat farm?" he asked.

"Really good, Toon, although, I must tell you she is not officially my girlfriend yet. Janice missed two weeks of school because of all the mud they had to clean up in the house and the barn. I brought her the daily assignments and took back her work."

Toon whistled. "What a lot of work getting a milking parlor back up and running. My dad had a dairy, and I always hated it. So things are now back to normal?"

"Pretty much," I said. "But as soon as the milking got back to normal, it was birthing season. There are six sets of twins this year which is surprising."

Grandpa winked at Toon. "Must be because of all that good feed that Orin had to buy what with that mud still on the ground."

I collapsed on the chair. "What good does it do to have more goats, though, since they are going to have to sell or move them when the development starts in?"

"Oh yes. Checkmate! Gotcha, Toon!" Smiled grandpa. "Lyle, you want to play?" said Toon.

I knew what to say. "Sure, but you will probably beat me."

"Aw, never mind," said Toon, waving his hands in the air. "So tell me who owns that land that they've been wrangling about?"

"The parcel with the big swamp is owned by the Cofelt family," said Grandpa. "I think Fred won it in a card game back in the '40s. Another big parcel is owned by the former mayor."

Toon made a funny face. "Oh, him. Ummmm, well that is the way of the world," said Toon as he got up. "Everything is up for speculation to make big bucks, and then they move away. No one cares about the people that are already there or the good of the community. Nowadays they spend ten thousand dollars on each election wearing everyone down, then they just take it from you."

Communication

Pushing the clouds away, the wind was ready to clean out the old dim winter chill and bring on summer. One day as I came home from school, I opened the front door, and the screen door blew up against the wall and ripped off the top hinge. I took the old rusty chair and propped up the door then grabbed the door handle of the front door and gave it a shove. The door was stubborn, but then popped open. There was grandpa in his chair, asleep.

He started a bit, but when the door slammed shut he sat upright and looked around.

"Oh hey, Lyle. I'm glad you are home. Your mom got called in to work at Home Depot, and Teddy is at Madge's with Milly and Billy." He yawned.

"Is Baby Mary there too?" I asked as I put down my backpack.

"No, she's here. She has a really bad cold. Snot running down her chin. I don't know how she got so sick," he said as he cast his eyes around the room.

CRASH... TINKLE TINKLE... BOOM BOOM... WAAAAAAA!

It was from Baby Mary and sounded like it was coming from the kitchen. I ran in, past a partially pushed down baby barrier. In the kitchen, there was broken glasses and plates all over the floor with Baby

Mary in the middle of it with a tablecloth over her head. I took the tablecloth off of her and grabbed her up, as she yowled. She had no clothes on—not even a diaper and her nose was streaming. I wiped her up and inspected a pile of clothes strewn on the floor. Most of them were wet, so I put her on my hip and got a diaper and some new clothes.

Then the phone rang. "Grandpa! Could you get the phone? I'm sort of busy here," I said as I wiped her face and got a T-shirt on her chest.

The phone kept ringing, so I started into the living room with Mary and a diaper and the rest of her clothes. When I got to the door, I saw that grandpa got it.

"Hello, hello? What are you doing waking up an old man?" said grandpa. "Is that you, Toon? What do you mean you can't hear me? I got my hearing aids in. Put your hearing aids in. I can hear you, you can't hear me." Suddenly, grandpa's hearing aid started squealing into the phone. He pulled it out and threw it on the floor. "Okay, can you hear me now?" Obviously grandpa could because he was listening to Toon who was talking pretty loud.

"Lowe, why don't you get some new hearing aids? I've told you a hundred times!" shouted Toon.

"Oh, okay, can you hear me now?" said Grandpa.

Toon was bellowing into the phone. "You couldn't hear me not me hear you. For Criss-sakes! Anyway I got some great news!"

Grandpa looked at me, and I felt like I was eavesdropping, so I went back to Mary's bedroom and finished dressing her. I turned on the space heater and some soothing music and rocked her to sleep. I warmed up her "blankie" at the space heater, wrapped her in it, and lay her down in her crib. Then I went back to the kitchen to clean up the mess.

The Beast in the Yard

One more week of school and my sophomore year would be over! I stayed up until 2:00 a.m. studying for the Biology final, and I was pretty stoked. I was up early because it was a day to walk to school. Then the phone rang.

It was Janice. "Lyle you've got to get down here! We have an emergency! A bulldozer just pulled up to our porch! I mean like right up to our front steps! Our first step is crushed!"

I could hear Janice's dad, Orin, yell to Janice, "Janice! Call the cops—NOW!"

Janice was weeping. "Lyle, get everyone here to witness—Call Madge—Call everyone." She hung up.

Biology final forgotten, I called Madge and woke up Mom. Everyone—Mom, Grandpa, Teddy, and Baby Mary—were loaded in the car, and we zoomed down the road to the goat farm. The big tractor trailer that hauled in the bulldozer was sitting by the side of the county road. We followed the bulldozer track that widened the lane by a foot on both sides. Bushes were crushed in its wake.

There was Janice's folks arguing with this big man in a plaid shirt and rounded shoulders. Arlo was on the porch, and Janice was in the doorway of the house on the landline phone with 911.

We all got on the porch by climbing over the bulldozer blade while the shouting was going on. Madge came roaring in with a truckload of people, including Shad.

He lifted Billy and Milly up over the bulldozer blade and onto the porch. Arlo brought out a bunch of toys and Legos for the kids to play with. Madge joined the shouting match with the bulldozer driver who waved papers in everyone's face.

"These people have a right to a thirty days' notice to vacate their rented property!" shouted Madge.

"Don't they read the papers?" yelled the driver. "This property is gonna be a subdivision, and we have to get all the trash from the flood cleaned up."

"Really?" said Orin. "Well then, why weren't you here months ago when we did clean this place up? Are you inferring that we are trash?" With that he swung his fist at the driver, but the driver ducked. Then the cops arrived. Three carloads of them.

Even though it was Janice that called them, the cops acted like we were the bad guys immediately, and this poor guy with the bulldozer was being bullied. It would have been hysterical, but we were too mad to really notice.

The head cop swaggered over to the bulldozer and climbed over it. He got on the porch and looked over the children and adults on the porch. There were ten people on the porch, and now the cop made eleven.

"We must get you all out of harm's way, so I'm going to ask you all to leave the porch," said the cop.

"Why?" asked Teddy.

The cop looked at my four-year-old brother. "Because we are going to tear down this house with the bulldozer. Don't you want to watch that?"

"No," said Teddy.

Janice was still on the phone to 911 because they don't want callers to hang up. "You know what?" she said into the phone. "I called your cops to protect us, and they want us to get off the porch to tear down our house. I don't call that protection at all, so fuck you all and goodbye." She threw the phone down and sat down on the porch and started to cry. I went over and sat with her and hugged her. We all just sat there, pretty silently.

The cop turned to us again. "I will warn you one more time. You all must get off this porch. The children will be physically taken off the porch. The adults will all be arrested. The children will be put in protective services."

Madge, Orin, and Violet all got on the porch. The porch groaned with the weight. Orin started singing, "All we are saying is give Peace a chance." We repeated the line over and over locking arms and sitting down.

The cop chose the smallest child—Baby Mary. He picked her up under her arms and at arm's length carried her to the edge of the porch and handed her to a cop down below. Baby Mary started screaming bloody murder.

She kicked the cop's arms with her muddy boots. The cop started to haul Baby Mary away. Then they grabbed Teddy and he went down kicking and screaming.

"You are traumatizing our children!" shouted Madge as she whipped out her iPhone and started videotaping.

They put Baby Mary and Teddy in a squad car and came back for Billy and Milly. They started screaming too and Billy bit the cop.

"We will sue you for not having children's seats in your vehicle!" shouted Mom as Madge kept on videotaping. In the meantime, the lights in the squad car came on followed by honking followed by the siren. The cops carrying Milly and Billy raced to the car, but Teddy, being resourceful, locked all the doors from the inside.

While the half-a-dozen cops were looking for car keys and holding little kicking children, we started chanting: "No More Bulldozers! No More Bulldozers!"

That went on for about twenty minutes, and the bulldozer driver was making a video with his phone too. My head was throbbing from all the noise and stress. Then, suddenly, a miracle happened.

Up the lane came a big white Cadillac. A lady with a cloud on her head got out of the driver's side. When I squinted my eyes, I saw that the cloud was her hair. It looked very fine and puffy. She looked like an angel with a color coordinated cream and white outfit. Toon Waldo got out and loped along beside her and two guys in suits got out. They all looked strange standing there in the dirty yard. The lady waved a bunch of papers in front of the cops and the bulldozer driver.

"I am Mrs. Louise Colfelt, and these are my lawyers," said the angel. "This gentleman here now owns this land. It is all legal."

Toon took over. "Okay, as owner of this land I order you to move this bulldozer off my property. This ordeal is over and you," he said as he pointed to the cops, "are free to go."

The cops put Milly and Billy down, and they raced back to the porch.

The cops seemed relieved as they released the kids from their patrol car and left. The heavy equipment driver climbed up on the bulldozer muttering under his breath. Then he yelled, "Get out of the way!" It was a fair warning as the huge beast started roaring its engine. It backed up and hit a tree, then dug a hole in the yard before it got down the lane.

"What just happened?" asked Madge as she hugged her kids.

Toon and Mrs. Colfelt looked at each other and gave a knowing laugh.

"Let's just say," said Toon, "that Louise challenged me to a game of chess, and I won!"

A View From The Top

We were free from the school routine. Free to roam around the countryside at least for a few days before grandpa dreamed up some farm work to be done or Janice's parents got her doing something with the goats.

"Mom and Dad think we should start up a 4-H dairy goat club." She said as she fought the wind whipping through her hair.

I gave her my baseball cap. "That sounds like a good idea." I said.

"Hey, Arlo, wait for me!" Yelled Teddy as Arlo suddenly sprinted ahead down the country road. Ever since the bulldozer ordeal, Teddy and Arlo have become good friends. Arlo is two years older, but they seem to be well-matched.

We hiked up the road to the rock out-cropping which I finally named "The Thinking Rock." This was Arlo and Janice's first time.

The boys were playing verbal "Land Skyler" by the time we got to the rocks and they were sitting on the rocks that were like high-backed chairs.

"Get back, Blowkiss!" Commanded Arlo to the invisible villain.

"Yeah! We will use our lightning bolts!" hissed Teddy.

Janice rolled her eyes. "Jeeze! For two kids who have only played that video game like maybe two or three times and don't even own the game, you would think they coded it themselves."

Sighing, I said, "I know. Kids these days! They are so obsessed. Come around over here and you can see the view of the whole valley."

As we rounded the turn, Janice gasped. "You can see everything! 99W, the High School, Old Town... Oh look there is your grandpa's vineyard..."

"Great-grandpa." I corrected. "Yeah and see that green oval shaped area? That is your goat farm. In the winter you can see your house and the barn when the alders lose their leaves"

Janice squinted over to the goat farm. "That is just amazing." She said. "I wonder what it looked like 200 years ago."

"Take out all houses, streets, and farmed land and it would look pretty much the same." I said. "People have done the most to change the land. The land does not change that much over time."

"It would be strange, going back in time." She said dreamily.

"It is." I said a little too quickly.

She looked at me very strangely. "What do you mean by that?"

"Uh, well..." I hesitated. "It's a little dangerous. I would not take the boys with us if we went, but there is a place where we can go called 'Crack-In-The-Wall.' I'll take you there sometime this summer."

Janice laughed. "Lyle Kent, you are truly a mystery, you know that?"

I winked like Grandpa. "Maybe."